Michael Hardcastle was bor... shire, and after leaving schoo... he served in the Royal Army Educational Corps in England, Kenya and Mauritius. Later he worked for provincial daily newspapers in a variety of writing roles, from reporter and diarist to literary editor and chief feature writer. In 1988 he was awarded an MBE for his contribution to children's writing.

His first children's book was published in 1966 and since then he has written over a hundred more, but he still finds time to visit schools and colleges all over Britain to talk about books and writing. He now lives near Hull.

Other titles by Michael Hardcastle
and published by Faber and Faber

PLEASE COME HOME

Michael Hardcastle

faber and faber

LONDON · BOSTON

First published in Great Britain in 1995
by Faber and Faber Limited
3 Queen Square London WC1N 3AU
This paperback edition first published in 1996

Photoset by Avon Dataset Ltd
Printed in England by Clays Ltd, St Ives plc

A CIP record for this book
is available from the British Library

ISBN 0–571–17122–2

2 4 6 8 10 9 7 5 3 1

1

The moment they turned unto Anchor Avenue Rachel saw that all the curtains at the front of the house were drawn. 'Mum's DEAD!' was the thought that overwhelmed her.

'Oh God, oh GOD!' she whispered and then, shedding her school bag, she ran to the familiar side-door, convinced now that her own life was as good as over.

Shelley, who hadn't uttered a sound, stooped to pick up her friend's bag and sling it over her free shoulder. For a few moments she didn't move at all, her fear of what news she might soon hear holding her back. In any case, she had neither the pace nor the urgency that possessed Rachel. Where, she wondered, had Mrs Blythe been found? In London? In Edinburgh? A nameless town? A river or a reservoir?

'Dad, Dad?' Rachel called softly as she looked first into the kitchen and then the dining-room where so often he was working on his account books. What sort of state would he be in? Would he be in tears at last? Would *she* have to comfort *him*? She'd never known that the beating of her heart could sound so loud.

She started up the stairs, holding on to the banister rail as she had never done before, fearful of what she was going to find: and still more fearful of what she would hear. Why, oh why, did she have to go? Why did she have to ruin everyone's life?

'Dad?' she again called softly, creeping up the stairs one by one. Then, perfectly distinctly, she heard the low hum of the Hoover; coming, she was sure, from her own bedroom.

It was, staggeringly, her father who was using the machine, calmly removing dust and debris from around the skirting board, operating with his normal calm efficiency: not many motes would escape his attention.

'Dad,' she murmured when she found her voice again, 'Dad, what're you doing?'

He looked up impassively at her as he held on to the door frame. 'Pretty obvious, I'd've thought. One of us has to do this job and if you're too idle then it must be me. Next time it's your turn. Don't wait for me to ask you, Rachel. All right?'

His free hand went to flick quickly through his thinning hair and at that moment she thought he looked his age.

'But – but – the curtains!' she wanted desperately to know. 'I thought – well, Mum, I mean . . .'

'I'm not having every busybody in this street watching what I'm doing,' he told her sharply, at the same time switching off the probing machine. 'This job's got to be done but I don't have to be seen doing it. I've got some pride left, you know, even if my wife has walked out on me, something that can't be concealed.' Somehow he kept the bitterness out of his voice.

Rachel moved into the room and weakly sank down

on to the foot of the bed, realizing her legs might not hold her up much longer. 'You know what I was thinking, don't you?' she asked him.

Her father shook his head. 'I never know what girls of your age are thinking. How am I expected to look inside your mind?'

That kind of remark was too familiar to Rachel for her to respond to it. It was the sort of thing he said, she believed, because he couldn't be bothered to work out a proper answer.

'I thought you'd had news that Mum is – dead.' She'd said it at last: the worst of all her fears was now in the open. 'I was convinced that's why the curtains were all drawn. Nothing else made sense.'

Again, he shook his head but there was no sign of any emotion. He might have been refusing another cup of tea or a request for a temporary loan. 'I told you, I just don't care to be observed.'

'So, there's no news? Nothing at all?'

'I'd've told you, wouldn't I, if there had been?' he replied matter-of-factly. 'I'm beginning to think it's time you stopped expecting it. If we'd been going to be told what she's done I reckon we'd've heard by now. It's getting to be pointless, keeping up your hopes like this. You'll just go on being disappointed. Best accept that you won't get any news. Then, if we do, well, it'll be a sort of bonus, won't it?'

He didn't mean it as a question and Rachel didn't treat it as one. Abruptly, she stood up and crossed to the window to draw back the curtains. Sunlight flooded the room. Mr Blythe blinked as if he'd been in total darkness until then, though there'd been plenty of light to work by because the curtain material was thin.

'Dad, do you really want Mum home?' she demanded. Sometimes, when she tried to be forceful in speech, he declined to answer. She knew he hated being 'backed into a corner by a wild boxer', as he put it. Rachel quite admired that choice of phrase because it was genuinely expressive. However, she never told him so.

He sighed. 'Well, of course I do. I mean, I wouldn't have to keep up with this housework lark, would I?' He paused but Rachel wasn't in the mood to respond to a good joke let alone a feeble one. 'Listen, just because I don't keep weeping into my tea and screaming and yanking my hair out – what's left of it – well, it doesn't mean I don't care. Don't know why you suspect I don't care. Because I'm guessing that's what you're thinking. It's just that, well, I feel pretty hopeless, as you do.'

Rachel thought of saying something about that but decided against it. She wanted to hear what else he might say. For once, she'd caught him in a mood when he might be willing to communicate. Perhaps the horror of the housework could be swapped for a worthwhile discussion.

'After all,' he resumed a few moments later, 'we've been married nearly fifteen years, a hell of a lot longer than many couples last. We've always got on pretty well, just the odd little tiff about something or nothing. Never had a real blazing row. Well, you should know that, Ray. You've never heard us shout at one another, have you?'

She shook her head because it was true. On the other hand, she wasn't with them all the time, was she,

4

so how did she know what they did or said to each other when they were on their own? Neither of her parents, though, was exactly the emotional type, more the opposite. They were inclined to keep their feelings under control at all times.

'So I'm just as much in the dark as you are about why she's gone,' he went on sedately. 'I'm just as mystified as you are about where she's taken herself off to. If I had a crystal ball I can promise you I'd use it. I want, I desperately want, to know where she is. That she's safe, in no danger, even happy, if you like. Though that doesn't seem entirely fair to me because she's definitely made us unhappy by just disappearing like she did. But, as I say, I don't for the life of me want to imagine she's suffering in any way.'

He paused for breath, leaning now for support against the built-in wardrobe door but still clutching the sucking mechanism of the vacuum cleaner. Rachel couldn't remember hearing him say so much in one speech. Fleetingly, she felt a trifle guilty for stirring him up so much that he shared his feelings with her so nakedly.

'But she's been gone for three weeks so if she wanted us to know what she's up to she'd've found a way of getting in touch by now, wherever she is,' he said, almost as if speaking to himself this time. 'Somebody must know where she is but they're not letting on, are they? Very likely your mother's convinced them that it's in her best interests not to tell us. She must have given 'em pretty good information of some sort or other to do that. Can't for the life of me imagine what it is, though.

'No, it's useless, really, thinking about it. Thinking's doing no good at all. If thinking would – '

'But that's why we've got to do something practical, Dad!' Rachel charged in. He was becoming thoroughly exasperating again. 'Wondering will get us nowhere, we've proved that already. Can't you ask the police again, *plead* with them, to start looking properly?'

Her father shook his head defeatedly. 'We've been through all that time and again. You know the score, Rachel: your mother hasn't committed any crime just because she's left home. She's free – anyone is – to walk out at any time. There's no suggestion that anyone's kidnapped her or enticed her away or – or anything horrible. You know that. So the police are powerless to do anything. As that inspector told us, if the police devoted time to searching for every man and woman who abandoned their family they'd never have a spare moment to solve a proper crime. Police manpower's stretched as it is with so many things that really need their attention. So it's no good at all asking them again, it just isn't.'

Rachel's frustration was reaching the surface again like water from a burst main. 'Well, we've got to do something. We've a right to take some action, to find out what's really going on, haven't we?'

He sighed again. 'You've just got to accept that your mother's doing what she wants to do. Without us. That's what she wants. Otherwise she'd've been in touch or at least left a message. There's no suggestion of what the police call foul play, so what's happened is her own choice. You do see that, don't you? I mean, you're an intelligent girl. Your school reports say so.'

6

At other times Rachel would have protested about what sounded like a familiar jibe: but her mother's fate was all she could think about. Her instincts told her that her father's view couldn't really be challenged. Yet, unlike him, she couldn't sit back and simply wait for Mum, or someone acting on her behalf, to make the next move.

'We've got to do something, *got* to!' she repeated. 'This not knowing is driving me out of my mind. Honestly, it is, Dad.'

He gave her a sceptical look but that was all. His fingers hovered above the switch on the cleaner. As one day followed another he found he was thinking less and less about his wife, even though he missed her presence around the house. He was beginning to resent being forced to discuss her whereabouts even with Rachel.

'Dad, can't you think of *anything* we can do?' she asked, surprising herself with a plea to him for help.

'No. Nor can anybody else. I've told you that umpteen times.'

Before she could say anything else they both heard Shelley's voice, calling tremulously from the hall. 'Ray, are you up there? Is there any news? I mean, has your mum been found?'

'It's Shelley,' Rachel said unnecessarily. 'She's come home with me. We might go out for a bit tonight. Look, I'd better go down and tell her. She – we both did – thought the worst.'

Mr Blythe made no comment and even before she reached the landing he'd switched on the Hoover again. It did cross his mind, though, that now she was home he really ought to have told her it was time she cleaned her own room every week without fail.

'It's just Dad,' she told Shelley, pushing her gently into the refuge of the dining-room. 'Didn't want to be seen doing any housework, would you believe it? As if that mattered – I mean, his *image*. But it's what he thinks about. The "abandoned" husband!'

'So there's no news then?' Shelley, still uncertain what was going on, inquired.

'Not a whisper – par for the course, as old Simmy says every time somebody does something idiotic in his rotten old science lessons.'

Shelley sat at the table and propped her chin between cupped hands. 'Well, so it's not as – desperate – as you thought? You know, I was dead sure – oh, sorry! I mean, I didn't – '

Rachel laughed for what seemed like the first time that day. 'It's OK, Shell. I could've said the same thing myself.'

'Look, I could do with a drink if you don't mind,' Shelley said, as her embarrassment faded. 'Shall I get it? I – '

'Oh, sorry, sorry,' Rachel recovered. She should have remembered that Shelley always wanted something to drink when she got away from school. Neither of their mothers would have forgotten that. 'Tea? Coffee? Lemonade? Squash? Can't suggest anything stronger because Dad might come down any second.'

'Tea, thanks. After all, it's supposed to cool you down.' She watched, chewing the inside of her cheek, as Rachel filled the kettle, plugged it in, flicked tea bags out of a tin box into china mugs. 'Listen, did you hear what Lizzie Little said? I mean, I know she'd never say it to you herself.'

'Go on,' Rachel replied placidly, certain it would be no worse than some of the remarks passed by her school mates in the past fortnight.

'Well, she told Claire that she'd give anything, anything at all, if only her mother would disappear overnight! Said it'd make her life perfect! Can you imagine it?'

Rachel shrugged. 'I've heard a lot worse than that, Shell, so you don't have to spare me the sordid details. The prize offering was: "Well, I suppose it must be a bit worse than losing your favourite umbrella." That was Josie Kaye at her witty, witty best. In a funny way I suppose it was witty, though I didn't appreciate it at first. One or two of Josie's sickening mates laughed but a few others said they felt sick humour was a bit below the belt in this case.'

Shelley nodded vigorously, her chin still cradled in her hands. 'It was one of the postures she was trying to perfect for when she might meet a film producer. Her style and range of mannerisms would then be employed to full effect. 'You should just close your ears, ignore 'em all,' she recommended. 'I know I would.'

'No you wouldn't – you can't. If people want to gossip about you, they'll do it, whatever you say. And it's best to know what they're saying. I mean, it's like Mum being missing in a way. Knowing *something* is better than knowing absolutely nothing. Knowing nothing is torture. Well, it is for me. I don't know what Dad feels, or even if he feels anything.'

She glanced at the door into the hall but there was no sign of her father. She realized, however, that there was no longer any noise from the vacuum cleaner. Perhaps he was eavesdropping at the foot of the stairs. Momentarily, she thought of checking on that but then decided against it; what did it matter if he did hear what she and Shelley were discussing? It was all predictable and, anyway, he must know by now exactly what they thought about the situation.

It was perhaps the silence that drew him in, though he hardly did more than put his head round the door. 'Ah, hello Shelley. Nice to see you. How, er, are you?'

'Fine, thanks, Mr Blythe,' she responded cheerily, wondering at the same time if he would make some inane remark about what she was up to these days. Whatever she replied, he wouldn't listen to the answer, she knew.

'Was going to ask if you girls'd like a drink but I can see you've got what you need,' he said so aimlessly that Rachel knew he was criticizing her for not offering him one. 'Anyway, I'll leave you to your secrets. Oh, by the way, Ray, let's not eat too late. I may go out tonight. Need to see a client at his place for an hour or so.'

He withdrew and Rachel wrinkled her nose at her best friend to indicate her lack of interest. But Shelley's inventive mind was at work on another possibility.

'Perhaps he's going to meet your mum at a secret rendezvous,' she whispered, her dark brown eyes aglow. 'You know, they want to discuss the future without telling you anything because they need to keep you in the dark. They've got plans for you, though, because, you see, your dad – '

'Oh, Shelley, stop it!' Rachel said firmly, scowling. 'I'm not in the mood for one of your fairy tales. I know you're only trying to cheer me up but, well, the longer this goes on the worse it gets. I mean, I really, really thought the worst when I saw those curtains. Yet I also feel that any sort of news is better than nothing. Dad can't see that. He actually told me last night that the old saying about no news being good news is always true. Rubbish!'

Shelley dutifully assumed a solemn expression. 'OK, I understand that, Ray. But, well, what can you do? How can you find out something if nobody's got anything to say? Your mum's obviously done everything to cover her tracks.'

Rachel sipped her tea. 'The first thing I thought of when I saw the curtains and was sure Mum was dead was that there'd be a policeman with Dad to help him get over the worst. That's what usually happens if the police bring you dire news, they stay with you until someone in the family can take over, make sure you're not going to do anything mad like hang yourself or smash up the furniture.'

She paused, but only to gather her thoughts, and Shelley nodded to keep her going. 'Well, then I remembered that young copper, you know the one I told you about, with the little moustache to make himself look older, *feel* older probably, the one Dad and I talked to first when we reported Mum missing at the cop shop. He handed us over to an inspector but, well, I think he felt sympathetic towards us – me, maybe.'

Shelley nodded again, not wanting to spoil the

pattern of ideas. It would be foolish to joke that perhaps the young policeman had taken a fancy to Rachel because he liked young girls with green eyes and long legs. If she'd said that Rachel would have protested furiously that anybody could see she was much too young to have a boyfriend, even if she wanted one, which she definitely didn't. She always claimed she had a low opinion of boys, though Shelley doubted that Rachel had any real experience of them, especially as she was an only child. Certainly there was no boy at Torside School that Rachel had ever been seen to chat to in a purely social way.

'Well, I've got to do something and I think he could help. I mean, he must know about police procedures for finding missing people even if he's been a copper for only a short time,' Rachel went on quite animatedly. 'If he sees how desperate I am – we are – then I think he might agree to help. Just something, some advice on what to do next. That's better than nothing. So what about it?'

Shelley nodded slowly, although the idea didn't seem to have much merit to her. 'You could try it, I suppose. As you say, you've got to do something instead of just sitting moping. When d'you have in mind?'

'Tonight!' was the instant reply. 'You heard Dad say he'd be out. So he won't be checking up on where I'm going. The ansaphone can stay on in case Mum rings. You'll come, too, Shell, won't you?'

Her friend grinned. 'What're you going to do if he starts chatting you up, wants a date, *you* know? Won't want me around then, will you?'

Rachel frowned. 'Come on, Shell, this is serious, you know it is. You've been a great help so far, keeping my spirits up ever since it happened, standing up for me at school when people've been really stupid. Just being understanding. So don't start treating it as a joke now. That'd finish me off. I need someone to turn to.'

Shelley was contrite. 'Sorry!' She reached across the table to wrap her hand round Rachel's thumb and squeeze it. 'I suppose I'm just saying the wrong thing at the wrong time. Honestly, I do want things to go right for you. I care deeply about what's happened, Ray, I want to see you really happy again. I mean, we have great times, don't we, when things are going well?'

'So you'll come then? Tonight? Set off about, what, seven?'

With a kind of conductor's flourish Shelley got to her feet and raised her arms as if to invite the orchestra to stand. 'We'll go together and we'll return in triumph! It will be the first step on the rocky road to success. I swear it! Honestly, Ray, of course I want to be with you. Right, I'll get off home to show 'em I'm still around. Meet you at our usual spot at Sentinel Gardens at five to, OK? I promise, cross my heart, I won't be late.'

Rachel smiled a trifle wanly. 'Better not. I won't be hanging about because I feel in my bones that this time I'm going to get somewhere.'

2

Afterwards, it seemed to Rachel to be almost a miracle that Kevin McAtee was on duty just when she needed him to be there. Until she and Shelley scrunched across the loose gravel in front of the small suburban police station it hadn't occurred to either of them that the person they wanted to see might not be there. So, of course, they'd made no preliminary phone call to arrange an appointment.

'What're we going to do if he's not here?' asked Rachel, suddenly pausing in front of the midnight-blue door.

'Find out his name, when he *will* be here and come back then,' Shelley declared confidently. 'Or even get his phone number and give him a surprise call.' She was going to add more but, just in time, remembered her vow to stop teasing.

He wasn't in sight when they reached the counter, protected by a tall glass screen, but the smile from the sergeant on duty was welcoming. Rachel had expected a frosty reception, though she couldn't have explained why.

'Well now, I can't imagine two beautiful young ladies like you can have any problems for us,' the sergeant greeted them with exaggerated charm. 'Tell me you've found your way here by error.'

'Er, we, I, wondered if that young constable, you know, the one with dark wavy hair, bit reddish, I suppose – and the, er, little moustache – well, I wondered if he was here this evening.' Rachel stumbled through her explanation, watching the sergeant's eyebrows ascend. She mentally predicted that his flattery would now recede into sarcasm.

'Oh, I expect you mean Constable McAtee, young miss. That sounds a pretty good description of him. Is this call social or professional, I'd be glad to know?'

'Oh, professional, definitely. I mean I – we – need some advice about something, well, important.'

She knew that didn't sound convincing in the slightest but it was the best she could manage. She glanced sideways quickly but Shelley was impassive, as if none of this had anything to do with her. At least, though, she wasn't grinning or, worse, giggling.

'All right, then, if we can be sure you're not wasting police time I'll get him for you,' the sergeant said, in a matter-of-fact way. 'Could I have your name, please?'

'I'm Rachel Blythe and this is my friend, Shelley Kinsale.' She wondered if the man would write that information down in the large ledger he was studying but he didn't. To her surprise, he turned towards the door to his left and called out. 'Kevin, two of your admirers have turned up. They'd like to see you, if you'd be so good as to come out here.'

He emerged within seconds and his training in not showing surprise at anything he might experience in the course of duty proved effective. His expression didn't change at all when he saw who awaited him, rather to Shelley's disappointment. Perhaps, she reflected, he didn't remember Rachel at all.

'Hello, I'm Rachel Blythe,' Rachel announced again, taking the initiative without hesitation and smiling broadly. 'Don't know if you remember but I was in here three weeks ago with my dad to report that Mum was missing. Yes?'

'Oh yes, I think I remember now,' Kevin said with deliberate caution but without allowing his features to relax. The sergeant, he could see, was watching closely. 'What do you want? I mean, do you want to report she's been found now? Er, returned home?'

Rachel shook her head. It was going to be more difficult than she'd feared. Now she couldn't imagine why she'd supposed that this plainly inexperienced, almost bashful young policeman could help her. She was wasting her time, probably his time, too. She saw his gaze flick across to Shelley. Did he think she was older and more attractive? Did he prefer girls with brown eyes and short, dark hair? Immediately she was annoyed with herself for thinking in this way; what did it matter what Constable McAtee cared about? All that mattered was that he might be able to help her.

'Mum's not come back, no. We haven't heard anything at all. It's just as big a mystery as it was the day she left. Nobody seems to know anything and, well, we're getting pretty desperate.' She paused and PC McAtee's face at last creased into the beginnings of a smile of encouragement. 'So that's why we – Shelley, my friend, and I – why we thought the police might be able to help, just by suggesting something we could do. This not knowing's the worst thing of all.'

The constable exchanged glances with his superior but it was impossible for the girls to imagine what the men were thinking.

'Well, you see, I don't think we can do anything,' Kevin said eventually and there was a note of genuine regret in his tone. 'Nobody's committed a crime. Just by going away your mum hasn't done anything wrong. I mean, she might turn up any – '

'Yes, yes, I know all that,' Rachel cut in, fearful of hearing the same litany yet again. 'That was all explained to us and we do understand. It's that, as I say, we can't think of what to do next. We just need something to try. To stop the agony of our uncertainty.'

'I see,' Kevin replied slowly as if hoping that his sergeant would offer some advice. 'Right, what about employers, their connections? Your mum had a job, had she?'

'No. Not for, oh, at least a couple of years. And that was only part time in a shop, just to help out really.'

That question had been asked before and she'd steeled herself to say nothing about the flower-selling because Dad didn't want that mentioned. He claimed it was irrelevant and couldn't be of interest to anyone. She had an idea he was worried about the taxman knowing about the income, tiny though it was always said to be.

Kevin nodded and drew the tips of his fingers along the thin black line of hair adorning his upper lip. He knew all about this mannerism and believed his mother's comment that it made him look both older and thoughtful. 'Any relatives who might have heard something? During investigations the police often come across long-lost relatives nobody's thought to mention to us because they've been out of touch for so long, or because they've fallen out with one another and don't like to admit it.' He hesitated and then suddenly grinned. 'Sometimes there's been a secret making-up but it hasn't been mentioned to those left behind. Happens a lot, doesn't it, Sarge?'

The sergeant nodded but didn't say anything. It was as if he was seeing how his young protégé would fare when dealing with the public in a tricky matter all by himself.

'Well, we don't have any hidden relatives, any relatives at all, really,' Rachel explained. 'Dad's got an older brother somewhere in Australia but we don't keep in touch with him except for Christmas cards – and we don't always get them. Mum was an only one so that's that. Oh, and so am I. No brothers, no sisters.'

Shelley, feeling it was time to contribute something, however valueless, remarked chirpily: 'Dead unlucky, isn't she?'

Nobody responded to that at all, not even Kevin.

'Have you thought of advertising?' the young constable asked with a flash of inspiration.

'No thanks,' said Rachel deadeningly. 'Dad's all against that. Says it costs too much money and, anyway, it just lets everybody know your private business, doesn't it? Enough people know about Mum's disappearance as it is, he says.'

Kevin's supply of ideas now dried up completely. Biting the corner of his mouth, he looked towards the sergeant for support. It was forthcoming.

'Perhaps you could get your neighbours to put their thinking caps on and really remember if they saw anything unusual on the day your mum went away, Rachel,' he recommended in an unexpectedly gentle manner. 'And then you could also ask around the station, the railway station, and the bus station, see if anyone recalls seeing her get on a particular train or coach. You never know till you ask. People's memories are surprisingly selective but they need to be jogged. Our chaps would be asking questions like that if they were on a real investigation. Nothing to stop you employing their methods, is there?'

'Well no, I suppose not,' agreed Rachel, wondering whether she was really capable of going up to complete strangers to ask vital questions (vital to herself, anyway). She couldn't help looking towards Kevin, who was probably no more than five or six years older than herself. If only she could have had an interview with him in private then perhaps she'd've been brave enough to ask him if he'd be willing to ask such questions on her behalf. Interrogating members of the public was part of his life, she supposed.

The sergeant, misinterpreting her glance and suspecting that really she had other motives for turning up that evening at his police station, rubbed his nose rather vigorously. He was displeased by her lack of enthusiasm for his excellent suggestion.

'Apart from that,' he added brusquely, 'I don't know that you can do anything worthwhile. You'll just have to watch for the postman or stay by the telephone until your mum decides to get in touch. Or, of course, she could walk back through the front door at any moment. That's what usually happens and the missing person wonders what all the fuss was about. If she had a good reason for going away I'm sure you'll hear about it in good time, young lady.'

Rachel swallowed hard. 'We can't think of any reason, my dad and I that is, why Mum should have just walked out. I mean, there isn't any reason at all.'

The sergeant opened his mouth to respond but before he could utter a word Kevin blurted out: 'Well, maybe she has a secret friend, you know, a man, a lover, somebody nobody else knew about. And they just went away together. They've in love. I mean, it happens all the time . . .'

His voice trailed away as he sensed the effect his words were having on everyone. Rachel, he could see, was on the verge of tears; her friend simply looked angry, almost contemptuous.

The sergeant, eyes narrowed, frowning, said: 'We don't know about that, do we? Best to avoid speculation of that kind, Constable.'

The warning was clear. Kevin, shooting guilty looks at the girls, coloured slightly and murmured: 'Sorry, Sarge.'

'Ray, I think we'd better be going,' Shelley said gently. 'I don't think we're getting any further on here.'

Rachel nodded, thankful she didn't have to say anything more at the moment. Her heart was thumping, her emotions revolving like clothes in a washing-machine. One of her worst fears had suddenly been exposed. If her mother had run away with another man would Rachel any longer be in her thoughts?

'Listen, how d'you fancy a coffee, Ray?' Shelley

inquired as soon as they were out of sight of the police station. 'Let's just drop in at that new pizza place. I could do with something to wash the taste of that place out of my mouth.'

'All right,' Rachel agreed, allowing herself to be guided across one streeet and down another into the pedestrianized zone of stone slabs and circular plastic seats around colourless plants and a tangled metal fountain that was perennially dry. She wished she could go home alone and see if anyone had phoned and left a message. But she also needed Shelley's company and sympathy.

'Right, in here,' Shelley directed, heading straight for a table instead of obeying the command in the entrance space to 'Wait here to be seated'. Within seconds of their sitting down a young waistcoated waiter was in attendance, smile at the ready, pen poised over pad.

'We just want a coffee, that's all,' she told him sharply and put her arms around Rachel's shoulders.

'Er, you've got to order something to eat as well,' he pointed out with a weakening smile and a tremor in his voice. 'It isn't just, er, a coffee bar, this place, we're only allowed to serve drinks with food.'

'My friend here's just had some bad news, bad news about her mum. She's in a state of shock. So she needs a drink,' Shelley told him forcefully.

'Oh yes, right,' the waiter responded, jaw dropping as he turned to see what effect this shocking news had had on the tall, long-legged girl. He could tell that she was about to cry, or had just been crying. 'So what do you want? Coffee for both?'

Rachel nodded. Even as she reflected on the young

21

copper's words and how she felt about them she could admire Shelley's style, her manner of getting what she wanted and, moreover, *when* she wanted it. Yet she could also be extremely sensitive and discreet when it was essential.

Now, however, she dived immediately into the turbulence of Rachel's mind. 'Could she have gone off with someone else, Ray? I mean, how much do we know, any of us, about what our parents get up to when we're not there? Some mums have got all the time in the world to do anything they want. They're bound to have secrets, aren't they? Most things stay hidden for ever but the bits that get out are the bits the papers make a meal of. Front-page stuff, some of it.'

Her failure just to stick to her opening question allowed Rachel the time she needed to work out what to say. She knew she couldn't give a proper answer because she'd never picked up so much as the faintest hint that her mother had a 'secret' friendship with a man. Basically, Mum didn't seem interested in men at all, not even in Dad most of the time. Rachel thought it must be a very boring marriage from the way her parents related to one another. But then, most of her friends, her school-mates, said much the same about their own parents: those, that is, who still had two parents living together under the same roof.

'I can't believe it,' Rachel admitted eventually. 'I'm sure I'd've spotted, guessed, something was going on if it was. We've always been, well, it seems the only word, *close*. If something was bothering her, like Dad's moods or when he had that operation on his appendix, well, she'd tell me about it, even ask my opinion. And I told her everything.' She paused and added: 'Well, everything that wasn't a secret between you and me or something that she wouldn't approve of, like that day we bunked off to London to get those tickets for the Sin-Ko's concert.'

Shelley nodded but remained unconvinced by anything she'd heard so far. On other occasions Rachel had complained to her that her mother 'never tells me anything. She's got the idea she's entitled to ask me details about *anything* while she can hide whatever she wants in her life.' It wouldn't, though, be sensible to mention that now. Instead, she inquired softly: 'Well, what about the people who buy the flowers? Some of them must be men, getting them for girlfriends and wives. Maybe your mum got to know one of them. Look, I'm not suggesting anything, Ray. But, well, it *is* possible, don't you think?'

Rachel hunched her shoulders slightly. 'I suppose so,' she conceded reluctantly. 'But most of the people who take the flowers just leave the money in the honesty box by the gate. Even when one of us is in the house and somebody wants flowers they still put the money in the box, they don't come to the door. Don't need to, really, do they, because every bunch is clearly marked with the price. Mum always said that stopped any haggling. Otherwise people would just come to the door and offer what they thought the flowers were worth, or what they could afford, and then sometimes they'd get really abusive when they were told the proper price. Mostly it works OK. We don't get any hassle over them, and they don't get pinched all that often. Most people do seem to be honest; surprisingly, perhaps.'

She stopped as the waiter delivered small mugs of coffee to their table. He put them down with exaggerated care as if fearful of offending them should he spill so much as a drop. His eyes flicked towards Rachel to see whether she was still crying. When he saw she wasn't he didn't know whether to be pleased or indignant that the dark-eyed girl might have conned him. In a few minutes, he decided, he would return to see whether he could persuade them to order some food. After all, he couldn't expect a tip from serving just coffee.

'You know,' Shelley remarked after an interval of silence, 'I've never understood why your mum liked selling flowers in that way. It wasn't as if she was selling something she had grown herself, was it? Didn't she – *doesn't* she, sorry – buy them from somebody else? I've always thought it's a bit like being a shopkeeper without actually having a shop or getting to chat with customers. Just leaving them in buckets at the front of the house . . . well, what does she really get out of it? There can't be all that much money in it, can there?'

'Well, some days there're quite a few pounds,' Rachel said between sips of strong coffee. 'I even got Mum to lend me money from the flower fund, as we call it. You know, when I was a bit short. But I haven't a clue whether it's really profitable. Mum never talks about how much she pays for the flowers in the first place. Not to me, anyway.'

'So who does she buy them from?' Shelley persisted now that Rachel was prepared to discuss the subject,

24

previously something that was usually brushed aside whenever anyone mentioned it.

'Oh, just some man who likes growing flowers and has acres of room for them. But he's not very business-like, really. That's why he has several small outlets like ours instead of going to one big wholesaler. That's what most growers do if they haven't got their own retail place.'

'What's his name?'

'Ted Heywood. He's a really nice chap, kind and, well, a bit vague. Or that's the impression he gives. Mum likes him and so do I.' She paused as if debating whether to add more. Then: 'He gave me a job, actually. I quite like it.'

Shelley's widening eyes registered her astonishment. 'What! When was this?'

'Oh, a couple of weeks before Mum left. It's only for a few hours on a Saturday – well, Sunday if it suits me better. Doesn't pay much but he's easy to work for and he definitely needs someone to organize his correspondence and stuff like that. So . . .'

'You kept this a secret all right, didn't you?' Shelley remarked in an aggrieved tone. 'And I thought you shared all your secrets with me, Ray! How can friendship exclude something as big as this?'

'Hey, hang on! It's nothing great, honestly. As I said, it doesn't make me rich and it doesn't take up a lot of time. I didn't say anything to you, or anybody else, either, in case it didn't, doesn't, last.'

'So what exactly goes on, then?' Shelley inquired in a less challenging manner. 'How do you earn your measly pittance?'

'Oh, mostly keeping account books and correspondence up to date. Routine stuff, really, nothing thrilling. He's not methodical, you see, so he easily loses track of who he's promised flowers to and who should have paid last month and, well, whether he's even answered last month's letters! It's quite funny about his letter-box because it's not in his office or even near it. It's a sort of tin box on a pole at the entrance to his gardens. You must've seen American mail-boxes stuck up by their garden gates so the weary old postie doesn't have to walk too far, like in England. Well, Ted's is just like that. Sometimes when I go to open it it's stuffed full. He's very trusting about that because lots of the envelopes have money in, fivers and tenners as well as cheques, all payments for various orders. So I have to sort all those out and issue receipts.

'It's a nice feeling to be trusted and just left to get on with things in my own time. Ted himself just tends to the flowers. Sometimes the only way I get to see him is to take him a mug of coffee at the far end of the gardens. They're huge, you know, up on Grimscar Row.'

'How old is he?'

'Fairly ancient, I suppose, though he could be younger than he makes out. Be a pensioner soon, I imagine. Why d'you ask? Oh, I know: you think he fancies me, don't you? Well, forget that, Shell – he's old enough to be my grandad!'

Shelley smiled but didn't stop asking questions. 'Does he deliver your flowers himself, the ones that your mum sells?'

'Usually, yes, two or three times a week. He or his pal Bill, one of his neighbours, a farmer. They just drop them off when they come into town. We have an arrangement that they're just delivered to the back door or the shed if no one's in. It's always worked.'

She stopped and looked at Shelley under lowered lids: 'Listen, why're you going on about Ted? You surely don't think *he* has anything to do with Mum's disappearance, do you? He couldn't have, he's still here.'

Shelley shook her head vigorously, her dark hair swinging wildly from side to side. 'Definitely not! I told you, I'm just curious. I mean, your flower-selling – your mum's, then – it's something I've not really known about. But, well, it could be connected. Depends on whether your mum got invo– got to know one of her regular customers. Look, forget it. Sorry I ever mentioned it.'

She reached across to take Rachel's hand and squeeze it with affection. She wished she'd never raised the subject because Rachel wouldn't have started to cry like this. 'Ray, Ray, don't be upset – please! Listen, I'll – '

Rachel squeezed back. 'I'll be OK in a minute. Don't worry. I'm just – can't help getting upset when I think of everything.'

Shelley looked on sympathetically as her friend dabbed her eyes dry with a tissue and then, almost furtively, glanced round the restaurant to see whether anyone had noticed her unhappiness. Luckily, everyone else appeared absorbed in their own affairs, although the waiter, misinterpreting her manner, hurried across to inquire whether they were now ready to order food.

'I told you, we just wanted a drink!' Shelley replied aggressively. 'Is somebody queuing up for this table or what?'

'Er, no, you're all right,' the waiter stammered, discomfited by her manner. But he still had the professional presence of mind to scribble out a bill for two coffees and plonk it down on the table between them. As he returned to his station he wished the dark-haired girl would go to hell so that he could be the one to comfort her pretty friend. He would have made her happy again.

Rachel dabbed at her eyes, recovering faster than she'd imagined she would. Lately she'd dissolved into tears so many times she thought she'd drown in them (thinking up that phrase had made her smile in spite of the pain). But mostly she'd managed to keep them back until she was by herself. She'd never been able to cope with public displays of grief, her own or anyone else's. But Shelley was her best friend, her only really close friend, so shedding tears in front of her didn't matter so much.

'I sometimes think that might be what's happened,' she conceded in a low voice. 'But I didn't want to say so because that makes it seem more likely, somehow. There's got to be a reason why she went and, well, that could be it. But I haven't the faintest idea who he is – I mean, could be – well, *you* know. Don't suppose anybody else does, either, otherwise they'd probably have said. We certainly haven't heard any rumours about Mum and a – another man.'

She looked directly into Shelley's eyes to gauge her reaction. Until this moment she hadn't wanted to admit, even in her darkest moments, that Mum might have gone away with someone, possibly a flower customer, a man she loved so much (or thought she did) that she needed to be with him all the time to the exclusion of everyone else in her life. For that would mean that Mum loved someone else more than she loved Rachel. It would be the complete betrayal of their relationship as mother and daughter, 'the closest bond of all', as Mum had described it to her several times. 'Nothing should ever be allowed to damage that in any way.' Well, it was being damaged now and would suffer still more damage if Mum didn't return soon.

Shelley had been absorbing this new idea without rushing, as she usually did, into a quick response. She wondered how long Rachel had been aware that her mother might have eloped with a secret lover. It was an exciting possibility and Shelley didn't want to risk saying anything that would cause Rachel to refuse to discuss it any further, either because it was too painful for her or because she would decide it wasn't a possibility after all.

There were times when Rachel could infuriate her with her refusal to continue a discussion of an important topic just because she was afraid of saying too much. Prising secrets out of Ray could be as impossible as getting blood out of a stone, to quote her mother's favourite expression.

'Well, if she *has* found someone else,' Shelley started cautiously, 'I'm sure they'll have been spotted by someone somewhere. Not many people are good at keeping things secret for long, my nan says. Now how about the famous – sorry, *infamous* – Mrs Aries? I'll bet if anyone knows something it'll be her.'

Rachel's snort of annoyance was impressive. '*Her!* I'm not going to ask her anything. Wouldn't give her the satisfaction. You know that, Shell.'

'Yes, of course, but, well, sometimes you have to go against your own, er, principles just to get some advantage for yourself. You must admit, she takes an interest in you and your family so it's perfectly possible she knows something.'

'Even if she does I wouldn't dream of asking her,' Rachel replied firmly and dismissively. 'With luck, she doesn't even know Mum's gone. I think Dad and I've managed to keep up a pretty good front – you know, just carrying on as usual so that neighbours and other folk won't ask questions and get really nosy.'

'Could be, I suppose, that this man, if he exists, has got a wife who is also doing some wondering, wondering where he has gone and who he's gone off with,' Shelley mused on another tack. 'So she might turn up at your place if she's heard that he used to buy flowers from your garden stall.'

Rachel, pulling faces at the quality of the coffee, now wrinkled her nose at that suggestion. 'How's she going to hear about our place?'

Shelley shrugged. 'Dunno. But maybe in a weak moment or something her husband might have said where he bought the flowers he gave her every time he strayed from the straight and narrow. In all innocence, you know, never guessing he ought to have kept it secret because one day he might run away with – with – well . . .'

The finish was weak because she'd realized in mid-sentence that her conclusion was going to upset Rachel. 'Sorry,' she murmured. 'Just, well, had to work something out.'

Decisively, Rachel pushed aside the coffee mug and stuffed her purse into her pocket after putting some money on to the table to settle their bill. 'Listen, I think I'm all for getting off home, Shell. This place's a turn-off. Let's shift.'

Shelley, however, was anxious to keep Rachel talking because a new idea had just occurred to her, one that ought to be explored. If she let it go now, Rachel might refuse to discuss it another time.

'Hang on a sec,' she pleaded. 'I've just realized we might be looking at things the wrong way round, completely the wrong way round.'

Rachel sat back in her plastic seat again. 'How d'you mean?'

'Well, suppose,' Shelley ventured, speaking slowly, 'suppose your mum left because it was your dad who'd got – got a friend. Suppose she, your mum, told him if he didn't get rid of her then she, your mum, would leave. What if that's how it is, Ray?'

She watched anxiously as Rachel appeared to consider her latest supposition; but it didn't take long.

'How long have you been saving this up?' demanded Rachel, spots of pink appearing on her cheeks. She was struggling to suppress rising anger.

'What're you getting at?' Shelley asked in a tone of total innocence.

'Why? Why're you doing all this?' Rachel went on, her voice becoming louder, but not loud enough to alert other customers to the possibility of a developing row.

'I'm just exploring ideas, that's all, Ray. Don't get mad at me. We've got to talk about things. Much better to have them out in the open, surely. It's been three weeks since your mum left and we're still no nearer knowing anything, are we? You've said yourself it's a complete mystery. Right?'

Rachel nodded but didn't speak. She was willing Shelley not to say anything unforgivable. She had more than enough to cope with at present without losing Shell in a row.

'You see, I didn't want to say anything more until it seemed pretty certain she was not coming back,' Shelley went on, taking Rachel's silence as agreement. 'Every day since she went I've expected you to rush over and tell me she was back.'

'I did, too.'

Encouraged by that quiet admission Shelley went on: 'So as she hasn't come back and we still haven't a clue about why she went we have to think about all the possible reasons. So it could be your dad is the cause. We'll just have to try and – '

This time Rachel managed to get to her feet without changing her mind half-way. 'There is no "we" about it, Shelley. It's up to me to find things out, and I'll manage it somehow. But I'm not going around accusing my dad of doing something I know nothing about. Look, I've got to go. Loads of jobs to do. Most of the jobs Mum did fall on me now.'

Shelley sighed. Yet another discussion that promised to be really enlightening had come to a premature end because Rachel couldn't face up to the truths about her family life. No doubt Rachel would return home and mope about what had happened instead of tackling matters head-on and making positive moves to discover why her mother had left and where she was now. She certainly wasn't going to get any answers by sitting around and wondering.

The waiter seized what he knew would be his last chance. Dashing over to them he saw in a glance that the money on the table covered the bill (though included nothing for what he thought was exceptionally friendly service).

'Can I get you anything else? I mean, anything at all?' he asked in a fairly hopeless tone. He was looking at Rachel but it was Shelley who replied.

'Well, if you're a prince in disguise you can turn me into a princess! Otherwise, no deal,' she laughed.

Rachel smiled, too, though it wasn't the best of jokes; but she enjoyed the bemused expression on the waiter's face.

'I'll, I'll do my best,' he stammered, uncertain how to react.

'Oh, I'm sure you will, but it may not be good enough!' Shelley said, and swept out, her arm linked to Rachel's. 'Poor boy,' she added when they were in the street. 'He is not bad looking and it's obvious he fancies you.'

Rachel made no comment, eager now only to get home. When Shelley suggested that she should go round on Friday evening to see some new videos her brother was getting, she said she would. If one made promises to Shelley for future meetings she was usually willing to forget about the present.

'Don't start any new investigations without consulting me first,' Shelley demanded as they parted. 'Promise?'

'Promise,' Rachel agreed, knowing she wouldn't give it another thought.

Her father was still out, probably still auditing somebody's account books somewhere if he was running true to form. Although the tiny red light was flashing, indicating that someone had telephoned, there turned out to be no messages on the ansaphone. Rachel grimaced: either that was somebody who couldn't be bothered to speak to an impersonal machine or someone who couldn't entrust his or her message to whoever first listened to it in case that listener was the wrong person. As her father once remarked, ansaphones were complicated creatures with even more complicated lives of their own. They had a lot to answer for.

Feeling hungry, she made herself a double-decker sandwich from a small tin of crab meat and was beginning to feel better when the phone rang. In spite of the coffee she was sipping, her mouth dried up the moment she lifted the receiver. She was convinced she'd hear her mother's voice. Or, at worst, someone ringing with news of Mum.

'Is that Rachel Blythe?' inquired the male caller. A young voice. But familiar.

'Yes. Who's that?' she asked tremulously. It *was* some news, she *knew* it was.

'This is Constable McAtee, you know, at the station. You dropped in to see us earlier this evening.'

'Oh yes, yes.' What could he possibly be ringing her about? Had they heard –

'Sorry to be phoning you like this but, well, I wanted to apologize. I think, I *know*, I was out of order suggesting that your mum might have a secret friend, a man she'd run – gone – away with. I just wasn't thinking.'

Rachel was too surprised to say anything. Her mind was whirling with disappointment that it wasn't Mum, with relief that it wasn't bad news, with astonishment that the constable was taking the trouble to say he was sorry.

'Are you still there, Rachel?' he asked anxiously.

'Oh yes, sorry. I didn't know what to say. But thank you for ringing. Good–'

'Oh, hang on a second, please! There's something else. Just an idea I had, wanting to help you, you see.' There was a desperate tone in his voice now. 'You know you asked about trying to find a missing person, the police way, that is, and we said we couldn't help? Well, I can give you the name of a private investigator, if you like. Someone we use from time to time on undercover business where – well, I can't say much because we're not supposed to talk about it. But I'm sure he'd be happy to work for you.'

'Oh,' was all she could say. The whole conversation was becoming surreal.

'Yes, he's called Graham Taplow. Got an office in Wilton Crescent, number 22. He's in the phone book but I've got his number here if you can jot it down. OK?'

'Oh yes, thanks.' There was always a pen beside the memo pad and ansaphone so she didn't have to scrabble for one. She couldn't imagine herself ever ringing up a private eye to ask him to search for Mum but she wrote down the details all the same.

'Look, I've no idea how much a guy like him charges but I should think he'd be reasonable,' Kevin McAtee went on, gaining confidence. 'Sorry we can't help but, well, if you ever need any more, er, advice, you know where we are.'

'Thanks,' Rachel replied, hoping she sounded grateful because she didn't know whether she was.

'Right. Well, sorry again for saying the wrong thing. Hope you soon find your mum. Bye then.'

'Bye.'

She put the phone down. Had he rung because he really wanted to apologize – or had he been ordered to by the desk sergeant? She would never know; and, anyway, it didn't matter. Somebody had tried to help her: that was what mattered,

She was still thinking about the phone call when she got to bed. Would it do any good to try this investigator? Would he be capable of finding Mum? Would her mother *allow* anyone to find her? Suddenly, without warning, Rachel started to cry.

She wept for a long time. Then, eventually, she slept dreamlessly.

3

Janet Blythe hesitated outside the hairdresser's and then took a step back to glance along the narrow street before deciding whether to enter. It really was remarkably quiet, even for a Monday afternoon. Apart from a young man with a toddler pushing her own buggy and an elderly woman whose poodle was testing the water-resistant properties of a sapling it was deserted. As she'd walked along from the flat at the very far end she'd noticed no one peering from behind curtains or lounging by an open front door. Here, plainly, people kept largely out of sight. Whatever socializing they went in for, it wouldn't take place on their own front doorsteps. Whoever came by would hardly be noticed by anyone. Or so it seemed to Janet, who'd now ventured up the intriguingly named College Bath Road at least a score of times.

Crowning Glory was a distinctively modern name for what looked like an old-fashioned salon, and an ancient bell tinkled as she pushed open the door. It wasn't necessary in any way because the staff couldn't fail to be aware of any arrival; and, in fact, a solitary assistant looked up from her work to smile a greeting at Janet. She was young, black and assured in everything she did as she completed the tidying-up process for the customer about to leave. Janet had timed her arrival perfectly.

'Hello, good to see you,' the girl greeted her with a harbour-wide smile. 'You don't have an appointment, do you?'

Janet shook her head. 'No, I just dropped in, hoping somebody might be free.'

The width of the smile didn't contract so much as a millimetre. 'Must be your lucky day, then. I'm here and I'm free. Well, not for nothing at all, if you get me!'

Janet returned the smile but without the same enthusiasm, which would have been impossible for her, anyway. By now she realized the attention she'd get wouldn't be silent whatever else it was. Momentarily, she thought of leaving immediately. But her hair really did need doing and she might not again be so lucky with her timing. She'd simply have to do her best to curtail the conversation that now appeared inevitable. After all, she was the customer, so she could be brusque if she liked. She could even explain it away by saying she had a headache or, better still, a hearing defect. Who could argue against that?

'I'm Mollie,' the girl informed her as Janet slipped off her jacket and put on the proffered gown. 'Unusual, I know. But I like it. Folk remember it as well. Unusual, too, the spelling, "ie" at the end, not "y".'

It was, Janet guessed, a way of inviting her to disclose her own name, so that the encounter would be friendlier still. She resisted it.

'So, what is it you're wanting done?' Mollie asked after bidding her previous customer farewell and thanking her extravagantly for her 'generous tip'. She surveyed Janet through the mirror, the beaming smile still in place.

'Well, just a tidying-up, really. Hardly any shorter but, well, the ends tidied up. Definitely no highlights. I've always liked it as it is.'

'Not shorter, then?'

'Oh no! Nothing drastic, please.'

The beam brightened, if anything. 'Oh good. Long hair always look good on a tall woman. I hate to waste a good style, you know.'

Janet knew the conversation was about to become relentless but before she could cut it off Mollie changed the subject. 'You're not from round here, are you? I can always tell. Londoners aren't as ready to talk as strangers are. Local people tend to be a bit suspicious all the time. Visiting, are you?'

She closed her eyes in irritation: suspicion was precisely what she didn't want to arouse. 'Yes,' she answered in a clipped tone, hoping it would end the matter.

'Thought so,' Mollie responded serenely. 'Saw you the other day in the supermarket, All Hours, getting some fruit. Thought then it might be for a friend you were staying with, or maybe someone in hospital.'

This time Janet just stared up at the hairdresser, staggered that she had been observed previously and mentally noted in spite of the fact she knew she could have done nothing to draw attention to herself in any way since her arrival in the area.

'What – what made you remember me?' she asked, defying her own desire to stay silent. She had to know what mistake she'd made while trying to remain anonymous.

'You're tall, you know that, of course – and I wish I was,' Mollie replied. She laughed. 'And I know I'm not going to grow any more at my age! But it was your eyes, you see. Saw them when I was by you at the check-out. Never noticed me, did you?'

Janet would have shaken her head had that been possible; but at that moment Mollie was briskly washing her hair. It meant she didn't have to answer at all. Mollie took her silence for granted.

'Grey, a gorgeous grey, just the colour I've always admired.'

For a moment there was a pause and Janet felt she should fill it, say, perhaps (because it was the truth), that Mollie's own eyes were perfectly lovely. It seemed to Janet that the girl had nothing really to complain about; but then, she wasn't thinking objectively.

'What about your children?' Mollie wanted to know next. 'I'll bet you have a family, you look the sort. What colour are their eyes? Grey also?'

This is unbelievable, Janet told herself fiercely. She could have gone into any of a dozen hairdressers and she had to choose the one where the only assistant available interrogated you like a policeman grilling a murder suspect! Her luck must be completely out. If her hair had been dry she'd probably have got up and walked out in protest.

'Green,' she said aggressively, 'they're green!'

'Oh, lovely,' Mollie enthused. 'Couldn't wish for anything better. How many you got? Children, I mean.' And she giggled.

'Look, I'm really not in the mood to discuss my family, if you don't mind,' Janet told her in the same strong tone. 'I've got, well, a bit of a headache. So I'd rather just be quiet, relax, you know.'

'OK, no problem,' Mollie replied amiably, her supple fingers flicking quickly through strands of light brown hair. She didn't seem to mind being spoken to in such a sharp manner. Perhaps, Janet reflected, she's used to it if she tries to grill all her customers. Next time, she decided, she'd try one of the other places she'd noted among the network of streets that surrounded her flat in Barossa Square. Then, after some minutes of silence, Janet, feeling a trifle guilty, risked a smile. That change of expression was all the encouragement Mollie need- ed to revive the art of conversation before the drier rendered it impossible.

'Ever fancied the idea of living in London?' she inquired.

The question was so surprising that Janet took the bait. 'I did live here, once. A very long time ago. But – '

She stopped because already she'd said more than she wanted to say. She swallowed her chagrin at being coaxed into talking about herself again. But then, did it matter? Mollie was just somebody who obviously *needed* to relate to customers to do her job; doubtless she forgot everything she'd heard as soon as the next person sat in the chair.

'You know, I would never take you for a Londoner, no way,' Mollie sailed on. 'Don't strike me as one little bit like you'd ever lived round here.'

Janet closed her eyes in renewed dismay. What had she let herself in for now? Quickly she had to decide how to handle it: close the conversation down again for good or admit something that was unimportant?

'I'm *not* a Londoner, never was,' she said, choosing the second option because she was sure that Mollie was determined to keep up a flow of chat whatever response she received. 'I was just here for a short while, that's all.'

The next question, she was certain, was going to be about where she lived now; and she had an answer ready. 'Up north,' she'd say and refuse to elaborate on that. Doubtless Mollie would have some positive views on other areas of the United Kingdom.

'No, you see, I can tell you're really the friendly sort, which Londoners hardly ever are,' Mollie went on, proving herself unpredictable after all. 'I mean, I can just tell that you get on with folks when you want to. But if you've got a headache, well, 's natural you don't want to be jabbering away non-stop.'

The drying process mercifully prevented the need for any immediate response to that comment and Janet tried to work out what to say next. She also wondered whether Mollie had some hidden motive in keeping up a conversation like this. Was she, like so many people who worked in London, lonely? Was it a way of trying to strike up a friendship? Had she even sensed that Janet was a person with a problem, identity problems, that could be eased by sharing them with a stranger? It was impossible to answer satisfactorily any of those questions, so she wouldn't try.

It came to her, as she caught sight in the mirror of the girl's joyful expression, that Mollie was someone you couldn't help liking. Her friendliness, her willingness to risk snubs, was entirely natural. She hadn't once talked about herself, as so many people did, especially when they had a captive audience. Her interest in Janet seemed completely genuine. So shouldn't she reciprocate?

'You're not a Londoner yourself, I take it?' she remarked with the beginnings of a smile.

'Definitely *not*,' Mollie emphasized eagerly. 'From dear old Brum, that's where I started out – Birmingham to those who don't know the shortened version! But – '

'But you haven't got a Birmingham accent, well, not one that I can detect, anyway.'

Mollie was positively radiant now. 'Thanks. Well, you see, I wasn't born there, either, but it's more or less where I was brought up. But I can disguise my voice whenever I want because I'm really an actress, you see.'

Janet couldn't conceal her surprise. 'An *actress*? What're you doing here then?'

'Resting,' Mollie delivered triumphantly. 'That's what we call it when we're not actually in a show but just waiting for the next offer. Luckily, you see, I had training as a hair stylist, so, well, I just drop into it when I need the money.'

'Oh, well, that is useful,' Janet agreed, wishing she'd had training in something she could fall back on in an emergency. 'What sort of things do you act in? I mean, are you in theatre or TV? Must say, I hardly ever watch TV myself.'

Mollie laughed. 'Oh, you won't have missed me, lady – hey, listen, I don't know your name, do I, 'cos

43

you didn't have a booking. You know I'm Mollie, so, what's your name, if you don't mind me asking?'

'Janet,' she responded without thinking: and immediately regretted it. By now she should have learned to be prepared for the sudden inquiry and the need for a change of identity. At least, though, she hadn't disclosed her married name or her maiden name which she'd reverted to at the flat.

'Right, Janet, good to know you,' Mollie swept on. 'Like I was saying, you wouldn't have noticed me that much. All my parts have been little parts, so far. But I'm going to get there one day, you bet on it. I'll be in so many plays and comedies and, yeah, ads, that you'll all just get tired of seeing me. Then I'll be *really* selective, just do what I want, do what makes me the most famous person anybody ever sees, famous because of talent, I mean.'

'Good for you,' Janet murmured. It was impossible to tell whether Mollie was fantasizing or simply telling her true story. But there'd been a time when Janet herself had possessed similar ambitions: she was going to get to the top, she was going to be somebody the world would recognize and acclaim, she would always do what she wanted to do, not dance to someone else's tune. In her dream days she'd been younger than Mollie was now and the desires had been different in some ways. And then – and then it had all gone wrong and every hope for her brilliant future had been extinguished. Instantly. All because –

'Not boring you, am I, Janet, just pouring it out like this, like a river in full spate? I mean, you look a bit far away.'

'Oh sorry!' She really did feel contrite. After all, she had asked Mollie to talk about herself. 'I did say, didn't I, that I'd got rather a lot on my mind at present? And, well, I must get on with things at – at home. Loads to do, really. We must be just about finished now, aren't we?'

'Just about,' Mollie agreed, producing the customary hand mirror for the customary back-of-the-head view. When Janet smiled and nodded her approval she began to untie her gown. Her smile had faded.

'It's really very good,' Janet said in a heartily false tone to try to make up for the abruptness of her manner earlier. 'Thank you for fitting me in right away.'

Mollie shrugged. 'No problem. Hope you'll come by again. I've enjoyed talking to you.'

Janet added to the bill a tip that was more generous than she could afford; and it was big enough to bring the beam back to Mollie's face. 'Janet, thank you! That's really kind.' She hesitated barely a moment before adding: 'Look, if you fancy a drink together some time, and a *real* chat, well, I'd like it, really would.'

It wasn't at all what she'd expected and she was at a loss how to respond. Somehow, though, the interlude with the young hairdresser had brightened her outlook on things. She felt better for listening as well as for the haircut which, she had seen, was done very professionally.

'Right,' she smiled. 'I'll look forward to it, too, Mollie. We'll fix it up next time I come in, OK?'

Once again she saw from the tightening of the mouth that her answer wasn't as warm as Mollie had hoped: it lacked the definite promise of a date that she'd been seeking. Janet guessed that Mollie was wondering whether she was a victim of polite evasion.

She put her hand on Mollie's forearm as she opened the door. 'See you soon, I promise.'

As she walked along College Bath Road towards the flat she was sure that, if she turned round, she'd see Mollie standing outside *Crowning Glory*, watching her. Why on earth, she asked herself, did I have that effect on her when all I wanted was to remain anonymous? And what am I doing, helping to build a relationship from a casual encounter when I'm avoiding my own family, ignoring a daughter and a husband?

She walked on, faster than she usually moved, trying to suppress feelings of guilt that had been surfacing almost continuously since she'd arrived here. However much she'd hurt Rachel and Roy she *knew*, knew without even the faintest shadow of doubt, that she was doing the right thing, the honest thing. She was being honest to herself.

Turning a corner sharply, she almost bumped into a broad-shouldered man wearing a dark trilby and felt obliged to mutter an apology for failing to look where she was going. She sensed rather than saw the searching glance he gave her; and her heartbeat quickened as she hurried on. In an area like this it could be suicidal to speak first to a stranger, especially as any woman on her own these days was vulnerable even in familiar territory. She wished she dared risk a glance behind her to see whether he'd paused to look back at her. But then, if she did, would that be further encouragement to him to follow her? Janet bit hard on her lower lip and steeled herself to continue at her normal pace.

After a couple of no longer alarming minutes she slowed down and began to notice buildings again. This sombre brick was such a contrast to the brighter brick of so many houses in the north, yet it was often the case that the north was depicted by Londoners in almost stygian shades. 'From the frozen north, are you? The black country?' (which ignored the fact that the Midlands was not the north). 'D'you have to keep the lights on all the time?' they'd laugh, believing it was an original remark. And sheer disbelief: 'York less than two hours from King's Cross?' they'd exclaim when rail journeys were mentioned. 'You've got to be joking!'

Barossa Square was as deserted as usual at this time of the day and she wondered for the umpteenth time where everyone went. Hardly a single property remained in private hands; every house appeared to have been turned into flats whether three-bedded or single-bedded, whether for entire families or for those on their own like Janet herself. Yet she scarcely ever saw the same face anywhere more than once. Before crossing to number 7 she cautiously studied the openings and street corners, checking that no one was waiting there unobtrusively to waylay her. It had become a habit that made her feel what it must be like to have committed a crime that was recent and so far undetected. Of course, her disappearance from home was bound to be causing anguish and speculation; but she didn't believe anyone would have a clue where to look for her. None the less, she couldn't help worrying that one day someone would recognize her.

It was Rachel she was thinking of as she let herself into the tiny furnished flat on the second floor. At this time of day she'd be getting in from school, hungry for something now in spite of the fact that they would have a proper meal in only an hour or so; and she'd sit there, spooning up Weetabix and tinned apricots and sipping coffee and describing her day, lessons hated, lessons enjoyed, lessons endured, teachers who complained about this and unbelievably said *that* and demanded something impossible.

If there'd been a phone within reach Janet knew she'd have lifted the receiver and punched in the numbers she knew so well and so rarely had ever used. But the nearest phone was in Mrs Steadman's flat and she wasn't going to ask any more favours of her. Instead, she shook out her hair in the bathroom and concentrated, as she combed it, on what she was going to say to Helen when she saw her tomorrow. Then, if things turned out as all three of them were hoping, they could plan for the future.

4

'Gone away, has she?'

Rachel had expected a question like that the moment she caught sight of Mrs Aries hovering beside her garden gate. The brusqueness of her approach was unchanging whoever she was speaking to and whatever the circumstances. Not for the first time Rachel wondered how on earth Mr Aries, just supposing such a person ever existed, put up with it. But perhaps he couldn't, and that was why their neighbour lived alone.

'Er, just for a few days,' Rachel admitted cautiously, slowing down instead of trying to continue her brisk walk past the Aries' house.

'Not in hospital, is she?' the middle-aged woman inquired almost eagerly, her steely-blue eyes glinting with what could be anticipated pleasure. 'Didn't think she was looking too well the last time I saw her. Bit peaky, I said to myself.'

What she said to herself was Gloria Aries' favourite conversational offering: it was always her assumption that her listeners would want to know details of her inner dialogue. The phrase was invariably delivered with the weight of a scientific theory essential to the future of mankind.

'No, no, of course not,' Rachel replied dismissively in as lighthearted a manner as possible when facing the lowered brow and gimlet glance of the woman they'd been doing their best to avoid for the five years she'd lived in the same street. 'I mean, I'd know if my own mother was in hospital, wouldn't I?'

It was a mistake to adopt anything approaching a frivolous tone with the ever-serious neighbour. 'Oh, don't be too sure, my dear, don't be too sure. If she's away from you all and there's been no word, well, how can you be sure she's not met with misfortune and finds herself hospitalized?'

'Hospitalized' was a recent acquisition in her vocabulary and it suited her style, hinting as it did of depth of mystery and length of stay.

'What makes you think there's been no word from her?' Rachel counter-attacked spiritedly, confident she had made a telling point.

'Well, my dear, there've been no letters from her, have there?' Mrs Aries shot back with astonishing accuracy.

'How d'you know that? I mean, nobody knows. Except, well, the postman.'

'Indeed,' Mrs Aries agreed with a glacial smile of satisfaction.

'You mean, you *mean*,' Rachel said, quickly changing up a gear, 'you find out from our postman what letters he delivers to us? You ask him, and he tells you?'

The woman was not perturbed by this fierce doubt about the integrity of the postal service. 'Anthony is a dear young man,' she oozed in saccharine tone.

'Through all the dreadful weathers, hail, snow, wind, here he comes, right on time. The least one can do is offer him a little refreshment to reward him for his sense of duty. And there are times, you know, when even young men require – how shall I put it? Oh yes, that charming American expression – a comfort station.'

Rachel was only half-sure what this dreadful woman meant by that but she easily recognized Mrs Aries' ploy in diverting attention from one of her more outrageous acts by referring to someone else's problems and her sympathetic way of helping to deal with them. She wasn't going to fall into a trap.

'Listen, have you actually asked him what letters he brings to us? I mean, what's it got to do with you?'

Gloria Aries' hair was one of the fascinating things about her for it stood out at an angle from the sides of her head like slanted sails or corkscrew spokes from a wheel. It wasn't quite rigid but it remained at that acute angle without visible support or even, Rachel deduced, invisible lacquer. Her right hand would creep up behind it to assure herself from time to time that it was in place; it did so now but Rachel was too wound up to recognize that whenever she performed this gesture Mrs Aries was really playing for time because her lifestyle was under attack. It was not, naturally, because her conscience was troubling her. That never happened.

'My dear,' she said softly, meaning nothing of the sort, 'your mother is by way of being a friend of mine – no, listen please, Rachel. You asked me a question and I'm giving you an answer. Your mother I regard as a friend, someone whose well-being is a matter of concern to me, always. So when I became aware that she was, shall I say "missing", and I had no opportunity to ask you or your father, he being away so much himself in his line of business, well, I had to try other lines of inquiry. Perfectly natural, surely?'

Rachel found that hard to answer. Mrs Aries' confounded nosiness was a perpetual source of comment and dislike. It was laughable to think of her regarding Mum as a friend. Janet Blythe could be as scathing about Mrs Aries as anyone when she was in the mood to condemn. All the same, Rachel realized she felt a degree of gratitude, however tiny, that someone else cared about her mother's fate. Even her dad these days seemed to have written her off.

'Yes, but even if Anthony was able to tell you that we haven't yet had a letter from Mum how d'you know we might have been expecting one? Letters aren't the only way of, er, communicating, are they?'

Rachel felt pleased she'd thought of that argument, unaware that the real pleasure belonged to Mrs Aries. For their wild-haired neighbour could now be confident she was right: Janet Blythe had disappeared without telling anyone where she was going. Rachel had already confirmed Anthony's disclosure that, as far as he could tell, Mrs Blythe hadn't written to her husband or daughter. In his own way, Anthony was as inquisitive as Gloria Aries and never let a postcard pass from his bag without reading it. He took what he would call, if pressed on the point, a professional interest in postmarks and handwriting. So it could never be denied that on the matter of who received what through the post in Anchor Avenue and surrounding streets Postman Anthony was a genuine authority.

'Well, dear Rachel, if you're referring to communication by telephone then, of course, I accept that's possible,' Mrs Aries responded smoothly. 'However, I'm as well aware as you must be that your mother hates the telephone and can hardly ever bring herself to use it. A pity, but there it is. A phone call can save *so* much heartache . . .'

Rachel felt too wretched about Mrs Aries' hateful perception to think of replying that she and her dad didn't hate the telephone; and so *they* could have taken the initiative and rung Janet. Moreover, that would have given the impression they knew where she was. 'Look, I can't hang about, I've got to go and see somebody,' she announced abruptly. She was only wasting time; she was feeding the gloating ghoulish Gloria with glorious gossip. But she couldn't see any way of undoing it; her only recourse was escape.

'What about the flowers?' Mrs Aries asked with an unexpected change in questioning. 'It's a risk, surely, leaving them all day and every day with no one to answer the door or provide change for customers.'

'We can cope, thank you. We have done in the past and we'll keep on coping.'

'Such a shame about the flowers, though, just when things were picking up,' Mrs Aries meandered on as if Rachel hadn't said a word. 'She loved them so much, didn't she? All of them. But I'm sure her absence is only temporary, my dear, isn't it?'

Rachel had heard enough. 'Goodbye!' she snapped,

and swept away. She was at the end of Anchor Avenue before it occurred to her that she hadn't really handled that encounter very well.

She should never have admitted as much as she did and certainly shouldn't have rushed off just when the dire Aries was coming to the conclusion that Mum might have gone for good. What she should have done was appeal to her to say nothing about Mum's absence to anyone. It might have done no good but would have been better than leaving the enemy with advantages. At school Miss Kellett was always advising them to 'get people on your side, don't alienate them, don't give them cause to think you've anything to hide. Disarm your enemy with *charm*, with real honest-to-goodness charm. That way, you will finish on top, whatever their quarrel with you.'

Well, Miss Kellett wouldn't have been impressed with the way Rachel handled that meeting. She'd failed miserably. But at least it made her more determined than ever to conduct a successful interview with Graham Taplow, the only person left whom she believed could help her find Mum. He'd been willing enough to see her in the evening when she summoned up the courage to phone and ask for an appointment. Although she had misgivings about it, she was going on her own, sensing that he would be more likely to sympathize with her situation if she could present her case for help entirely by herself. Shelley would provide moral as well as physical support, she knew, but, on the other hand, Shelley was inclined to say the wrong thing at the wrong time, especially if she was bored by whatever was happening. There was, inevitably, a risk

54

in going to see a stranger in his office. To balance that, this Mr Taplow was a professional man and had been recommended to her by the police (even if the police were represented here only by Kevin McAtee). Anyway, he might have a secretary present to take notes.

Her original thought was to ask Dad to go and see the private investigator. After all, surely it was usual for the husband to initiate inquiries when his wife disappeared. But she knew almost exactly what he would say if she broached the matter directly: and was proved right when she tried a not very subtle hint instead.

'As the police say they can't get involved, do you think a private detective would be willing to try and find Mum?' she asked when he was watching the BBC news one evening and appeared perfectly relaxed.

'Oh, I'm sure they'd have a go if we asked one,' he replied, his eyes still on the screen. 'But it'd cost a fortune to engage one of those fellows, a *fortune*. You know I can't afford big money for anything.'

'Yes, but – ' Rachel was starting to protest when he cut her off, just as she'd expected him to do.

'Listen, I've told you umpteen times already, Ray. Your mum left of her own free will because, for some reason known only to herself, she wanted away. It's my firm belief that she'll simply come back of her own accord when she's ready. Until then, there's not a thing we can usefully do. I wish you'd understand that.'

What she understood was that he didn't want Mum home half as much as she did; maybe he didn't want her at all. Rachel had no way of knowing what he wanted; and, most of the time, she didn't care.

So she was on her own, 'as usual', she told herself. After making the decision to meet Graham Taplow her biggest problem had been choosing what to wear, though only someone who normally wore a grass skirt would be likely to describe her wardrobe as extensive. Her first thought was jeans and a T-shirt because she'd once read that men regarded most girls in jeans as sexless. Mr Taplow couldn't possibly be interested in her as a girl if that was how she dressed. But then, he would also immediately form a poor impression of her and her ability to pay his fee.

It couldn't be denied that she needed him on her side. Therefore she must make the most of her attributes while trying to avoid inflaming his interest in her as a female. Tricky, she acknowledged, especially as there was no one to ask for advice. The visit was a secret. Eventually she opted for the best she possessed: black skirt, cream blouse and her prized black velvet jacket. Only the ubiquitous jeans and T-shirt would have given her more confidence, though of a different kind. As it was, she felt she could meet any private investigator on level terms. Well, she could *begin* the meeting on level terms . . .

The plaque beside the bell-push was plainly and tactfully inscribed: Graham Taplow, Private Investigations: Confidentiality Guaranteed. It was reassuring that his office was on the first floor of a very ordinary-looking building which also housed a government department, an insurance company, a branch of the Inland Revenue and, rather more unpredictably, a chiropodist. Perhaps, Rachel grinned to herself, the poor old investigator and the insurance salesmen and the tax inspectors spent so much wearying time on their feet as they tramped around the town that they needed the comfort of a foot specialist when they returned.

Her worries about being entirely alone in a strange building with an unknown man were further reduced when she discovered that a security man was on duty at a desk in the foyer. Did some of the tenants work in the evening, then? She supposed that his presence meant they did.

'Yes, Miss, what can I do for you?' he inquired with agreeable courtesy as she walked in, though she was aware he'd already appraised her fair hair, long legs and skirt just above the knee.

'I have an appointment with Mr Taplow, the, er, private investigator.' She wished she didn't sound so nervous.

He nodded but didn't smile as she guessed he might. 'Very good. He's on the first floor, turn right out of the lift. He went up a few minutes ago so I know he's in.'

She rewarded his friendliness with one of her widest smiles and walked to the lift. It was while she was travelling upwards that the fluttering returned somewhere deep inside her and even checking her appearance in the mirror didn't help to allay it.

Mr Taplow opened the door within an instant of her knocking on it and, thrusting out his hand, he greeted her: 'You're punctual to the minute. I like that. Always shows character. Right, just follow me.'

It was said, she thought, as if he were a prospective employer interviewing her for a job; which was an odd way to begin a meeting where she was hoping to hire him. As she followed him from the empty outer office to an inner room which wasn't much bigger, it was his height, or lack of it, that surprised her. Even at her age she was a head taller. Her imagination had let her down quite heavily.

'Right, then, perhaps you'd fill me in with the details, sequence of events, when your mother left, what was said when she went, who she might have gone to, that sort of thing,' he said in brisk fashion. 'Don't hold back. I need to know everything if I'm to help you.'

He wasn't smiling or even looking particularly serious. He seemed to have no expression at all on his round face. To Rachel, studying him before deciding where to begin her story, Mr Taplow's face was a perfect circle, something she'd never seen on anyone before. His nose was short and broad and appeared to be underlined by the thin black line of a moustache. What colour his eyes were she couldn't tell, mainly because his lids were so close together. She wondered whether one of his parents might have been born in the Far East. In almost every respect, he wasn't at all what she'd expected. Fleetingly, she suspected he might have strayed into this office from the tax place elsewhere in the building.

From her bag she took an envelope and handed it to him. 'That's the note Mum left us. That's all we have to go on. She hasn't been in touch since, as I told you on the phone. We just don't have a clue about where she went or why.'

The investigator took the sheet torn from a memo

pad and held it up before his face. He read it aloud in a slow, solemn voice as if Rachel had never seen the words:

> 'I'm sorry I have to go away. Don't worry about me, I'll be all right. I'll be in touch again when I can. Love, Janet.'

He put the note on his desk with the sort of care he might give to a china cup, his lips pursed and his left forefinger straying to his moustache. 'So,' he said at last, 'this is your father she wrote to, I imagine. Nothing for you personally?'

Rachel was surprised. 'Well, no. I mean, I think the note was for both of us. Oh, I see what you mean, because it's signed just Janet. Well, sometimes I call Mum that – she says, used to say, it made us sound more like sisters.'

Sharp memories stabbed her emotions. Until this moment she'd managed to suppress the pain of not hearing Mum's voice since the day she'd left home.

'Right, then, I've got the picture,' Mr Taplow told her in his original businesslike manner. 'So fill me in on the rest, like I said.'

She didn't have to assemble the facts before presenting them because they were constantly in the forefront of her mind; and, in any case, she'd discussed them endlessly with Shelley. So she told of the astonishment, her own and her dad's, when they came home to find the note by the telephone twenty-four days ago. They were both positive Mum had given no hint to either of them that she was planning to go or had any reason to go. And no, she added emphatically before the investigator could ask the inevitable question, she and Dad were absolutely certain there was no other man in Janet Blythe's life. She had not run away to or with a lover.

She saw his lips tighten again, so she added: 'Definitely! There's no question of it.'

However, it was clear he was not convinced when he said mildly: 'Well, in all my years of experience of checking up on people I can tell you that it's often the husband and the rest of the family who are the last to find out when a wife's having an affair. Or the wife, if it's the other way round and the husband's done a runner.' He rubbed his nose vigorously and switched the subject: 'What about relatives she could've gone to?'

Just as vigorously, Rachel shook her head: 'Nothing doing there, either. Mum's parents are dead. I never met them because they died before she married Dad. She didn't have any brothers or sisters, just like me. Dad has a brother in Australia and his parents are in Germany and we know Mum wouldn't have visited either of them. Just to make sure Dad rang Gran to find out if they had heard anything from Mum. They hadn't. Honestly, Gran wouldn't cover up about anything like that.'

'Did your dad tell his parents that Janet had disappeared?'

Rachel barely hesitated: 'No. Dad wouldn't want them to worry about something like that, especially as they live so far away.'

'Any other reason?' he asked shrewdly. 'Such as not wanting to admit she'd walked out on him?'

It seemed pointless to Rachel to deny it, so she didn't. 'He really doesn't like people knowing Mum has gone, so he doesn't mention it anywhere if it can be avoided. I feel a bit the same but all my friends know, and most people at school, so I just put up with it when anybody asks or gets a bit nosy. Actually, most kids are sympathetic.'

He nodded as if he completely understood that situation but he didn't immediately put another question to her and Rachel wondered what he expected her to say next. She raised her eyebrows and said vaguely: 'I mean, that's what you'd expect, isn't it? That must be normal?'

Taplow gave no indication he'd listened to her. Instead, he asked abruptly: 'But what do *you* think is the reason for your mother's disappearance? You must have reached some conclusions about it in three weeks.'

She had known this question would arise but she still wasn't sure how to handle it. 'I've thought and thought and thought about it,' she began slowly, 'and I just can't work it out at all. It's a total mystery. I was, well, shattered when I got home and found the note and realized that Mum had really gone. Dad, too, was the same, though he doesn't show things as much as I do or Mum did   does, I mean.'

Pausing to work out her next sentence, she glanced up at him from under her brows. He was studying her impassively, twiddling a pencil between the tips of his fingers in the manner of some teachers. Rachel guessed she'd never be able to tell what was going through his mind.

'I think she'd become a bit bored with life generally – something like that, maybe,' she resumed. 'Restless, that's what people say, isn't it? You see, she didn't have a proper job, just selling flowers from the house. She had to organize that, get the flowers, see the supplier, but it took no time at all. Sometimes she sort of complained that she'd never been anywhere, never done anything, that she'd missed out on the good things of life. Also, she said not so long ago that when I leave school she'll have nothing at all because I'll probably move away. Most girls do. I know I will want to see something apart from Rocksea when I have the chance. But I've got probably three years at school to do so it's a bit early for Mum to be saying she'll be on her own when I leave. I suppose it could've been just an excuse, though, for her to go off and do something for herself now.'

She stopped because she felt she'd said enough and, anyway, wasn't sure how to continue without repeating herself. Mr Taplow was still twirling the pencil and watching her. Suddenly, he made a quick note on a pad in front of him and then, looking up, asked: 'Was she bored with your father, do you think? You said she was bored with life generally, so did that include him?'

'Yes, I think so. They didn't get on particularly well, in my opinion. Oh, they didn't have great, flaming rows like you see on TV. Might have been better if they did because then I'd've known what was bugging them both. They've never said much about themselves and how they feel when I'm around. Mostly it was just day-to-day stuff – how much to sell the flowers for, whether Dad would get home in time for supper, why he had to be out late again. He's an auditor, you know, checks people's, companies', balance sheets and so on. So he has to go out at funny hours when he's working for a one-man business or a shop or somebody like that.'

Rachel braced herself for what she was sure would be the next question. She was right. 'So your Dad could've been seeing somebody else? And that's why she left?'

'I have to admit, I don't really know, do I? I mean, it's not the sort of thing I would know because he'd keep it a secret. Mum never accused him of anything like that, I'm positive.' She hesitated and then went on: 'To be honest, I don't think he's that interested in women. He never talks about attractive girls or anything like that.'

She glanced at the investigator but he merely nodded for her to continue.

'My friend Shelley, well she says her dad never stops going on about women and girls that he fancies. He's obsessed with them. She knows he did have a girlfriend a few years ago but his wife – Shelley's mum – well, she just forgave him. Shelley says there're lots of men like him and you can always recognize them because of the way they look at females on TV or on the street or anywhere. I'm just as certain as I can be that my dad's not like that, and I'm not saying it because he is my dad. Mum once told me she was his first girlfriend and he promised he'd never want anyone else.'

'So how do you get on with him?' Taplow inquired in a conversational tone.

'OK, I suppose. He's not always telling me to do this or do that or ordering me not to go out to see friends or restrictions like that. Easy-going, that's how I'd describe him. He keeps himself pretty much to himself and it seems to be his policy to let others do the same.'

He changed direction, swivelling his chair at the same time. 'Have you ever suspected your parents might have money troubles?'

She shook her head. 'Doubt it. We're not loaded, nobody I know is, but we seem to pay our way without any hassles. I mean, we've managed without Mum having a job. The flower sales don't amount to much, according to both of them. I always get my pocket money on time and if I need something desperately – you know, for school or a new top or new shoes or something like that – well, I can rely on them to find the money.'

'Both of them, or is it your dad or your mum who gives you the cash?'

'Dad.' She was emphatic until it occurred to her he might make a false interpretation and suspect her mum was inclined to be mean with her. So she quickly added: 'Mum would always help if I had a problem with Dad, or if he wasn't around and it was an emergency. Then she'd find it somehow.'

He nodded but made no other comment. For once, he didn't ask another question right away and Rachel realized he wasn't sure how to continue the interview. So she looked away, concentrating temporarily on a shelf of books above an old-fashioned heavy metal safe. They looked as dull as the rest of the office, the sort of books someone opened only if they were three parts bored to death: thick, weighty in every way, dusty, deadly. Probably they were for reference only. Taplow gave the impression he would find his answers by talking to people, not consulting books. Was there, she wondered, a gun in the safe? She'd never seen one, apart from rifles at fairgrounds, and it occurred to her an 'automatic' must be an interesting object. Had Mr Taplow ever shot anyone? Killed him? Wounded? You never could tell about people –

'Sorry?' She realized he'd asked a question and she hadn't been listening. Or, if she had, she couldn't quite believe she'd heard correctly.

'I said, do you have a boyfriend?'

Rachel blinked, she couldn't help it. What on earth had this got to do with anything they were talking about at present? As she sat down in the chair indi-cated after entering the office she'd been aware that he glanced at her legs; her skirt, she knew, had ridden up a few centimetres above her knees. Men always snatched a look at your legs whenever the chance arose. Instinctively, her hands moved to ease the skirt down a fraction. And she felt herself colour up when she saw that he knew exactly what she was doing – and probably thinking. Oh hell, she told herself, this is becoming stupid. I should never have come, never.

'No,' she told him, sounding rather prim to her own ears. 'But what's that got to do with my mum?'

Taplow shrugged. 'Could be several things. Main thing, though, is that you're younger than you sound-ed on the phone. Much younger, actually. I hadn't suspected that I was going to be asked to represent someone under age.'

'Oh.' Perhaps she'd misjudged him after all. Perhaps he wasn't attracted to her in the slightest. Just as well but . . . She attempted a smile but she knew it didn't come off. 'Does it – well, make a big difference?'

He leaned forward, half-way across his desk, looking for the first time rather menacing, certainly intimidating. She could imagine how a suspect would feel when Graham Taplow was beginning to pin him down with unchallengeable details of whatever crime he'd committed.

'Have you the slightest idea how much an investigation of the sort you're talking about would cost?' he put to her.

'Look, I've got money in my building society account,' she responded swiftly. 'Been saving like mad for ages. For a special holiday or something. But if it helps to find Mum I'll spend it right away, all of it.'

'How much are you talking about?' he said crisply this time.

'Two hundred pounds – more really – there's the interest and – '

He laughed, not cynically but with evident humour. 'Do you know, Rachel, what that's worth? Not even a day's work in an investigation of this kind, and that's before we start totting up expenses. Just think: your mother could be anywhere in the world. And I'd have to make my way there to check her out, follow up clues, hints, wild ideas that people have. Think of the cost of getting there: car journeys, train fares, taxis, even planes. Paying for nights away from home – and I don't believe in slumming it in dicey digs, I can tell you.'

He gave her a moment to see how she would react: or perhaps to let all that sink in. Then he added, killingly: 'And nobody, nobody, has any clue at all as to where she is, from what you tell me. Could be anywhere in the world, as I say. So nobody has any idea how long it'd take to locate her. Minimum of a fortnight, I'd say. So minimum of fourteen daily fees; and it could take half a year, if you let it. Rachel, we're talking of possibly thousands of pounds in hardly any time at all. Relatively speaking . . . '

Rachel heard the pun but ignored it; she didn't know whether Mr Taplow knew he'd made one and she didn't care. She didn't care, either, how much of her knees was revealed when she sat back in her chair, sighing with a disappointment she couldn't hide.

'I'm sorry, Rachel, really sorry,' he said unexpectedly. 'I do realize how much it means to you to find your mother. I understand your determination to get the right sort of help. Unfortunately, I have to earn a living. I'm not a charity.'

She hadn't imagined he had such kindness in him. She had seen him as tough and thick-skinned and without much heart at all. 'Thank you,' she said, feeling tears gathering behind her eyes. She stood up quickly, not wanting him to suppose that she burst into tears to wring free help from him. 'I'm sorry I wasn't, well, what you expected.'

He rose, too. 'Oh, don't bother about that. In this work you meet all sorts and get used to winning some, losing some. It's always a gamble, you know, being a detective. You practically need second-sight to be successful, just like you do if you're backing a racehorse.'

She was leaving without having made a centimetre of progress along the road, the mysterious unmarked road, to where her mother now resided. She had gained nothing, nothing at all. Yet . . .

'Look, Mr Taplow, can I ask just one thing, even though I'm not in a position to pay anything for your services?' she asked, turning to face him. 'I'll understand if you can't give me an answer. But, well, what can I do now?'

His smile faded as he realized she wasn't leaving immediately. He felt he'd been more than generous already after he'd seen how young she was (though, these days, it was nearly impossible to tell from her general appearance whether a girl might be thirteen or eighteen). But, in his job, he was used to having his time wasted in a variety of ways; he was used to being patient. And, you never knew, sometimes a casual word made all the difference to solving a problem or changing someone's life.

'Look,' he said in a kindly tone, 'this would be a hard case whoever took it on, me or your best police brain. From all you've said, there's so very little to go on. As your mother didn't have a regular job she won't have any employment documents or anything in that line. You say there's no relatives so she can't be traced through them. You say she gave no hints to you or your dad and so she was probably very confident she could hide herself where she liked without risk of being followed. Really, Rachel, I'm sorry but there's no worthwhile advice I can give you.'

So it was no good after all. He had, she recognized, done as much as he could in the light of the fact that

68

he wasn't going to earn as much as a penny out of her mother's disappearance. But nothing was going to make her give up her quest. She held out her hand to say goodbye – and to put what had to be her final question.

'All right, I accept all that and I'm truly grateful, Mr Taplow. Honestly. But, and I swear it's the last thing I'll ask, if you were getting a million pounds to solve this case from someone who meant everything to you, well, where would you start? Just one hint, that's all I ask!'

He shook hands perfunctorily, sighing deeply as he did so. 'It'd have to be the neighbours I'd try first. They're the sort of people who sometimes know more than they let on. You might strike lucky, or just unearth some tiny nugget after plugging away for ages. You never know. And now – '

'Thanks for everything,' she called over her shoulder, and dashed for the lift. It was waiting for a passenger and she turned as she entered it but Graham Taplow had already firmly closed his door behind him.

Neighbours, she was thinking as she reached the street, neighbours! What did they know? What could they disclose about anything to do with the Blythe family? Mrs Aries was the only one who displayed interest in them and only that evening had showed herself to be as much in the dark about Mum's whereabouts as Rachel and her dad. It was obvious the private detective was so anxious to be rid of her he'd said the first thing that came into his mind.

Her depression was stealing back. She could feel it

settling on her again. More than anything, she needed to talk to a friend, someone who cared about her, Shelley.

Finding precious coins in her purse, she searched for a phone and was thankful that when she located a kiosk it wasn't in use. 'Be there, be there, Shell!' she urged as she waited for a response.

'Hello, who are you?' the child's voice came surprisingly confidently down the line and Rachel realized she'd got one of Shelley's younger sisters.

'It's Rachel. Is Shelley there? Look, can you be quick because I'm in a public call box. Is that Simone?'

'No, no, wrong again! This is Lucie. I thought you'd know me by now, Ray.' The child bubbled with laughter. 'You never do, do you, when you ring us up?'

'Sorry – I can't be perfect, you know!' Rachel replied irritably. 'Anyway, there are so many of you, how can I be expected to work out everybody's voice?'

'Well, I know *yours*, I always know you're Rachel,' Lucie went on serenely and, to Rachel, increasingly irritatingly. 'So, I think – '

'Look, is Shelley there or not?' Rachel cut in, aware of her money disappearing as each second went by. 'I need to know *now*.'

'No, she's gone to the big, big supermarket with Dad and Mark. I think she wants Dad to buy her something, 'cos normally she won't go anywhere near the place. That's what Mum says. Do you know where it is, Ray? It's – '

'I know nothing,' Rachel told her bitterly. Shelley's absence was the predictable end to a less than perfect evening. But she managed to say, 'Bye, Lucie, sorry

I've run out of money,' before she replaced the receiver
and headed for home.

5

With increasing annoyance, Janet watched the child
trying to fit the square peg into the round hole: the
classic dilemma being acted out in front of her for the
first time in her life. In spite of trying to knock the
plastic peg into the hole for the umpteenth time in
succession Sebastian refused to try another one in the
hope of succeeding. The toy, designed as an aid to
learning, was plainly teaching him nothing. Yet, to
Janet's surprise, he displayed no irritation himself,
simply a remorseless determination to win eventually.
Any normal child, she thought, would have become so
furious with failure by now he'd've hurled the toy as
far as he could throw it.

She sank back into the cushions of the gaudy green,
gold and blue sofa and made a conscious effort to curb
her adult disappointment at what was going on. Of
course, Sebastian was quite normal; there was really
nothing wrong with him and at times he could be good
company – when, for instance, she read to him or
allowed him to watch something noisy and colourful
on TV. Maybe, she reflected, small boys always
possessed such painstaking persistence; perhaps that
was a trait they needed to get on in life later, to win

through as a male. Would she have been more sympathetic to such behaviour if she'd had a son? Impossible to say, of course: but it was something she wondered about from time to time. If she'd had a son, would her life have been any different? She didn't think so. Now in other cultures it mattered vitally to give birth to boys, not girls. Girls were said to be a sign that the Gods, whoever they might be, were not on your side. If they could be got rid of quickly, so much the better. If she'd had a son could she have abandoned him at a crucial point in his life as she'd abandoned a daughter? She shook her head with the uncertainty such a question posed. She'd never know.

'Oh, Sebastian, give it up, for goodness' sake!' she exclaimed when exasperation at last overtook her. 'Look, I'll put a tape on, then you can have a dance. Like that?'

Dancing was, surprisingly, one of his greatest enthusiasms and his mother was convinced he'd take a leading role in a film musical at a tender age. It was probably the only habit he had in common with Rachel. She'd liked to dance and sing at the same stage of childhood, but it didn't last; at school she resolutely refused to sing a note on her own and would only consent to sing along with the rest of the class when her teacher threatened her with exclusion from the Christmas concert if she kept up such mulish behaviour. Nowadays Rachel denied that had ever happened if Janet tried to raise it as an amusing anecdote in conversation.

What, she couldn't help conjecturing , was Helen like at that age? Did she find it fun to sing or dance?

She must remember to ask her. Another question to ask. There was so much she didn't know, even about the basic facts of Helen's life.

Sebastian hadn't listened to her. The square peg was still being jabbed hopelessly at the round hole. Was there something wrong with his hearing? She hadn't really suspected that before but it could account for his liking the music to be so loud. Had Melody, his mother, ever had worries on that score? She must find a way of asking her, diplomatically, of course.

Melody, no doubt, would instantly deny that there could possibly be anything at all amiss with her beloved only child. Janet was discovering that was one of the problems of child-minding: telling Mum what her child was really like when Mum wasn't present. If something had gone wrong then the instant reaction was that it was the child-minder who was at fault. So it was best just to report at the end of the day, or half-day, 'Oh, everything went perfectly. Sebastian was as good as gold.' (Why, Janet sometimes pondered, was gold always said to be good? Just because it was valuable? Yet often in life it was the inexpensive pleasures that provided the best value. Ah well.)

'Sebastian, *stop*!' she ordered at last, physically removing the square peg from his grasp. He permitted it without protest, probably because by now he really was bored with that preoccupation himself. 'Shall I put a tape on for you? To dance to?'

He shook his head quite violently (another sign of hearing difficulty?) and instead pointed at the TV set placed on a shelf so that it was out of his reach. 'Story,' he said, 'picture story. NOW!'

Janet looked at her watch, though she knew precisely what time it was. Melody's orders were that her son should watch no more than two hours of TV per day, and one of those hours was allocated as a pre-bed ritual that was outside Janet's jurisdiction. Another half-hour was allowed over and around breakfast so that Melody, a single parent, could get herself ready for her secretarial role in the office of a film distributor. Melody believed passionately that as long as she looked at her best every day of her life then the man of her dreams (she actually referred to him in those terms) couldn't fail to notice her whenever he chose to materialize. So, she declared gaily, she always needed 'that breathing in and out space before I set off to work'. Thus, Sebastian could see TV for no more than half an hour during the time he was with his minder – and Janet had had to promise, hand on heart, that under no circumstances would she extend that period of viewing by so much as one minute.

'There's nothing on you'll like,' she told him, though she knew she was really speaking for herself. None the less, she switched on and Sebastian's timing was rewarded by the happy sight of cartoon characters in animated action. Janet, who'd allowed him glimpses of a programme earlier, would have to switch off in ten minutes or break her promise, something she'd hate to do. So her only hope would be to pacify him with food for he was sure to start wailing when his entertainment was removed, wailing that could go on destructively for minutes on end. It had been so much easier with Rachel for she loved being read to and would listen without interrupting to any story which caught her attention. And the library thus became as familiar as the corner shop to Janet.

Almost at once there was a scene of a character speaking on the telephone – and automatically Janet glanced across at Melody's cream-coloured mobile telephone handily placed on the high old mantelpiece of the Victorian living-room. The temptation to ring Rachel was stronger than ever. Surely one quick call couldn't jeopardize all her plans? There was a chance she'd be home from school now. Janet needed to hear her voice again.

While still keeping an eye on the child she was minding she previewed the conversation she might have with Rachel, who would immediately demand to know where she was speaking from; that was inevitable. Janet decided the only fair answer was, 'I can't tell you. I'm at a friend's house,' because that wasn't a lie; Melody might be paying for her services but she could be regarded as a friend. Next, Rachel would demand to know when Janet was coming home. 'I can't tell you when yet but I *am* coming back to see you, I promise.' That was going to be the most difficult sentence to utter because Rachel was sharp enough to notice that she (Janet) didn't use the word home and that she only spoke of 'seeing you'. But what else could she say? At present she had no idea at all of how things would develop with Helen; and therefore she had no clear idea of what her own future would be.

Her aim must be to ask Rachel about herself, to find out how they were coping without her, if there'd been any major problems caused by her sudden departure, whether anyone – well, the police, she meant – was actively trying to find her. Because she'd checked the point anonymously through a telephone call to the Citizens' Advice Bureau she knew that no one could accuse her of any crime simply because she'd left her family without telling them why or where she was going. But now she needed to know that they weren't suffering in any respect.

Of course, Rachel was probably dismayed but her mother still couldn't predict whether she would be bearing any emotional scars as a consequence of her absence; Rachel was good at covering up her real feelings, always had been; she didn't say much, she complained very rarely about anything. Was that, Janet wondered, because she'd failed her as a mother, because she hadn't encouraged her to express her feelings and she hadn't displayed the love she felt for the child when she was small? How could she tell if any of that was true? How could any mother really know if or how she failed her own flesh and blood?

Sebastian gurgled with pleasure and Janet's attention switched to the screen. It really was quite a funny scene with this ridiculous dog being chased through a farmyard by a very woolly sheep and upsetting other animals as they went by with, astonishingly, an elephant wielding a hedgecutting implement in its trunk lumbering in pursuit. Sebastian was intoxicated and Janet was able to resume her interior dialogue with her daughter. Rachel was sure to demand a chance to see her, not least because Rachel had always wanted to travel, to visit exotic places, to meet 'new people', as she put it. Most young people, Janet supposed, were like that and it had to be admitted that, as a family, she and Roy and Rachel had never been adventurous, they'd never even gone to another sea-side town for a holiday. That, perhaps, was one of the limitations of living on the coast: the sea and its allied attractions were not a novelty, so you didn't need to experience them elsewhere. Exotic? She smiled at her recollection of that word of Rachel's. Well, it was hardly likely she'd consider Barossa Square 'exotic' if ever she saw it. Still, it was certainly different from the house on Anchor Avenue.

She looked at the clock: one minute, well, two min-utes at most, and she must switch the TV off, whatever Sebastian's reaction. So, if she was to do it, she must ring now. She was in the act of reaching out for the phone when, amazingly, it rang. Her arm froze for a moment, unable to move, as she listened, still aston-ished, to the phone's curious pip-pip-pipping. Then she had the good sense to turn and lower the volume on the TV so that she could hear the caller. Sebastian scowled his displeasure and Janet hissed urgently: 'It's only while I'm on the phone. Don't worry. Won't be a minute. Probably a wrong number.'

It wasn't. It was Melody, ringing from work. 'Hi, Janet, how's it going? How's my little angel?'

'Oh, fine thanks, Melody. Everything's fine. I was just going to read Sebastian a story.' Janet crossed her fingers to counteract the baleful influences of that lie. There was a significant pause before Melody spoke again. 'That the TV I can hear in the background?' She had ears like a spy's listening device and Janet should have remembered that and reduced the volume still further.

'Definitely not,' she said positively. 'Sebastian's been enjoying himself too much to want to watch TV. Is there, er, some interference on the line at your end, Melody?'

Janet could visualize Melody's sharp shake of the head. She did nothing by halves.

'Oh right,' she responded unconvincingly. 'Listen, I just wanted to know if you could do an extra hour tonight – stay on till, well, seven, no later, I swear. It's just that we've been asked to do overtime, the paperwork for this late extra order. Don't want to let the firm down, you see.'

'W-e-l-l,' Janet murmured, not wanting to refuse and yet knowing that an extra hour here would leave little margin before she saw Helen. And she couldn't, for the world, be late for that. It was why she was here.

'I'll pay you, naturally – bit extra, if you want it,' Melody said hurriedly, misinterpreting the hesitation she heard.

'Oh no, it's not that,' Janet told her, again not absolutely honestly (and in that answer she knew how much her life and philosophy had changed since she decided to come here on perhaps the most vital mission of her life). But money was important to her: child-minding and cleaning jobs were the only way she had found to supplement her savings without being asked by employers about National Insurance numbers and tax offices and official forms. 'It was because I've got an important engagement tonight and can't risk being late for that. So – '

'Janet, don't worry! I won't be any later than the hour, I swear on my little angel's head. Listen, I've got

Kevin almost standing over me with a stop-watch! Must get on, right. Janet, thanks a million. I know I owe you and I'll make it up to you. Bye. Oh, and a million kisses for my angel.'

Janet put the receiver back with a double sense of relief. The call was finished and, by a small miracle, she hadn't been trying to ring home when Melody phoned and found her own number engaged. If that had happened then Melody would be bound to have suspected that her child-minder used her phone surreptitiously whenever she felt like it, never mentioning it and never offering to pay the cost. So dare she risk it now? Sebastian was still enslaved by the increasingly chaotic farmyard chase and it was long odds against Melody phoning again within a few minutes especially if her boss was standing in front of her desk. Really, there wouldn't be a better chance than this, perhaps for days.

Janet punched out the numbers without delay. So often, in recent weeks, she'd been on the point of ringing, only to change her mind at the last moment. If Roy answered, which was perfectly possible though not probable at this time of day, she knew what she'd do: put the phone down immediately.

It rang – and rang – and rang. And no one answered. If there was no one in the house then it was strange the ansaphone wasn't on. She wouldn't have left a message but at least she'd've known the house was empty. Perhaps they'd simply forgotten to switch it on this morning.

'Oh Rachel, darling, what're you doing at this moment?' she asked herself, needing to hear a familiar voice, even if it was her own. 'I don't know when I'll be able to ring again, when I'll have the nerve, the strength. Oh Rachel, pick up the phone.'

But still no one answered.

At last, she had to replace the receiver. Almost instantaneously, the crazy cartoon ended. Janet switched the TV off, stifling Sebastian's protests by picking him up and heading for the kitchen.

'Come on, let's get you something to nibble,' she told him. 'Just because I'm having a bad day doesn't mean you've got to have one, too. But you'd better be good until your Mummy comes home because I'm not going to be in the mood to give in to you all the time. So, be good, Sebastian! And I promise I'll try to be good, too, in spite of the way I feel.'

6

Rachel was adding up the sums of money she'd found in the mail-box that morning when Ted Heywood shyly put his head round the door almost as if he felt he was an intruder.

'Any news, love?' he inquired and Rachel knew from his tone that he was referring to her mother.

' 'Fraid not,' she replied with a half smile.

'Well, I think I have,' he told her quietly.

She was astonished but still had the presence of mind to switch her calculator off. He wasn't a man to make jokes under any circumstances and so whatever he was going to tell her demanded complete attention. 'About Mum?' she asked, hope audibly triumphing over disbelief.

He nodded as he stepped into what Rachel called his office and he still described as The Shed. 'She wants you to know that she's all right, she's well and, oh yes, that there's nothing to worry about. She'll be in touch with you direct as soon as that's possible.'

She stared at him, transfixed. 'Mum's telephoned you?'

'Er, I didn't say that, Rachel, no, love, I didn't say that. I've just had, well, a communication from her.

Very brief. Nothing else, no other message!'

He looked embarrassed but she was sure it wasn't because he was concealing something important. After working for him over several weeks, and even though she saw him for only a couple of hours at a time, Rachel knew that it was difficult for him to talk about anything of a personal nature. He really was just about the shyest person she'd ever met. His weekly inquiries about her mother were always of the gentlest as if he worried about adding to Rachel's pain simply by mentioning the absence.

'But – but,' she stumbled, trying to formulate a question. 'But did she write, then? I mean, she must have if she didn't telephone. So where did she write from? Oh, please Mr Heywood, I've got to know. Not knowing anything at all has been driving me mad!'

His gnarled brown hand pushed through his surprisingly luxuriant mass of silver hair, another sign of his general agitation. 'I can't tell you that, Rachel, I just can't. You see, love, I can't break faith with your mother. I do understand how she feels. I also understand how you feel. But, well, the thing is, your mother's entitled to her privacy when she asks for it. We all are, come to that.'

Rachel had tried before, and failed, to get Ted Heywood to change his mind. Once he'd decided on something, whether it was personal or business, he wouldn't shift a millimetre in any other direction. She couldn't, for instance, understand how he could manage without an answering machine when he spent so much of his time in his gardens out of range of his telephone bell. He owed it, she tried to persuade him, to his customers to be more accessible. 'I've managed for umpteen years without one and I'll manage in the future,' he pointed out. So he obliged them to use the post instead when they couldn't call on him in person. And because his prices were so low, his customers accepted his eccentric ways.

Now she tried to think of a way of outflanking him, of getting the information she desperately needed without Ted realizing he was giving it away. 'When did this letter arrive?' she inquired brightly. 'Couldn't have been today because I opened all the post.'

'I didn't say there was a letter, Rachel,' he replied with the merest hint of a smile to show he'd detected her ruse.

'But you didn't say there wasn't,' she shot back at him in some triumph. 'Did you?'

He gave a sort of half-shrug and began to turn away until Rachel quickly went on: 'Mr Heywood, do you know that this is the first word of any kind we've had from Mum? We have not known whether she's alive or – or dead. Whether she's gone abroad, even. She could've done anything. So, well, any snippet of news, however tiny, is precious. So, please . . .'

This time he faced her as she spoke. 'Rachel, love, if I could help you, I would, you ought to know that. I'm very, well, fond of you and your mother. You've both been very helpful to me and I wish I could reciprocate. But, you see, I've told you all I can and that has to be that. If your mother wants you to know more next time then I'll be glad to pass on anything I can. Glad to.'

For the moment she stored away the most vital piece of information he'd just given her and changed tack. 'Was the message just for me, Mr Heywood, or did it mention Dad? I mean, I can tell him, can't I? I'm sure he's just as worried as I am.'

There was a pause before he answered but his expression gave nothing away so she had no idea what he was thinking about; perhaps he regarded it as a more important question than she intended it to be. 'I'm sure you should tell him what you can, Rachel, just what I've told you,' he said carefully. 'I'm sure he is worried, we all are. But at least we know now that she's well and thinking of us all. That's a comfort, isn't it?'

The tears were starting behind her eyes and so she just nodded instead of speaking. It flashed through her mind that if she began to cry, openly, then Ted Heywood might be moved to tell her more. A lifelong bachelor, he'd probably find it hard to cope with tears and so might be sympathetic to whatever she needed.

'Yes, it is, thank you. Thank you for letting me know the news,' she said quietly and solemnly. 'I'll let Dad know and, who knows, Mum might write to us next time.'

She watched closely his reaction to that remark and felt rewarded when he nodded quite briskly and said: 'Yes, she might. I hope she does, Rachel.'

She knew then, was absolutely positive, that he'd received a letter from Mum; and, what also seemed certain, that he'd been told she'd write again. Her instinct told her not to mention that conviction.

All the same, she decided to risk one last question. She allowed her hand to reach for the calculator so that it appeared she was resuming her work, that their conversation was over. In that way, she might catch him off guard again.

'Mr Heywood, just one last thing please,' she requested, letting her voice break before adding the last word. 'Did you, well, get the impression that Mum's on her own? Or do you think she's with someone?'

He bridled at that and Rachel knew she'd made a mistake. 'I'm sure that's none of my business, Rachel, definitely not. I wouldn't dream of asking about such a thing, even if I were talking direct to your mother.'

This time he turned away abruptly and agitatedly fiddled with a ball of twine and then a pair of secateurs on the shelf opposite her desk. It wasn't in his nature to tidy anything up so Rachel half-hoped he was trying to make up his mind whether to add something to his previous comments. On the other hand, perhaps he was trying to come to terms with the idea that Janet Blythe might have run away with another man, someone he, Ted, actually knew, such as a customer of his. But Rachel recognized that even if he did believe such a thing were possible, Mr Heywood would never admit it to anyone. She'd always heard the description 'prim' applied to various women; but it occurred to her now that it perfectly suited the silver-haired old gardener. Could there ever be a greater contrast between him and the lip-moistening prying of Gloria Aries?

'I'll see you later, before you get off home,' Ted promised her, hurrying away.

She wished she'd apologized. The last thing she wanted was to upset him in any way. Suddenly he had

86

become her link with Mum, her one hope of being able to make contact with her.

Somehow she had to find a way of persuading Ted to reveal Mum's whereabouts; or, best of all, to show her the letter or card he'd received. She was convinced the message had come through the post. And so, she'd also convinced herself, would the next one. Ted had more or less admitted that when he had said something about 'the next time' and promised he would pass on any further news.

For the present Rachel found it impossible to concentrate on the work she was supposed to be doing. Her mind was in turmoil as she tried to decide what she should or could do next. There had to be some way of finding out where her mother was, there *had* to be. But she knew it would be impossible to get Ted to disclose the vital information. His sense of honour would never allow him to betray any promise he'd already made to Janet; even if it wasn't actually a promise he'd given he'd still feel he couldn't reveal anything without first seeking her permission.

Rachel jumped to her feet, too restless to remain at the desk. Like Ted before her, she fidgeted with the various objects on the shelves: twine, old seed catalogues, the rusty secateurs, several old jam jars containing seeds or bulbs and even, in one case, the discarded skin of a large spider; but although she tried to tidy them into straight lines or neat piles her mind refused to be organized in similar fashion. She couldn't even decide what to tell her father or even tell him anything at all. If there'd been a telephone to hand she'd have rung Shelley to ask what her best friend could

87

advise. But possibly that would have been a waste of time, too; these days Shelley was tending to keep a distance from her. The only reason she could think of for that was that Shelley had found a boyfriend, one she wasn't prepared yet to talk about to Rachel.

It was no good. She couldn't come up with any solutions at all, however hard she tried to force her intelligence into rewarding channels. Her one brilliant idea she daren't pursue: for it suddenly occurred to her that the only way she could get the information off Ted was to knock him out and then go through his pockets until she found her mum's letter! She was sure he'd've stuffed it into a pocket after reading it for he was the last man in the world to file anything for future reference, as she knew from working for him. Methodical was a word he'd probably never heard in his life. Similarly, it wasn't his habit to throw anything away that might have a future use and so it was extremely unlikely he'd have ripped the letter into little pieces and flushed them down the loo or put them into a waste bin. So there was no doubt in her mind that the letter still existed. The only other way she could get hold of it would also involve committing a criminal act: breaking into Ted's house while he slept and searching until she found it. 'Don't be ridiculous!' she told herself.

She forced herself to abandon her scheming and all thought of her mother and to concentrate on her work again. The sooner that was finished the sooner she could go home and make realistic plans. When, three-quarters of an hour later, she had done all that could be done, she hurried down to the far end of the sloping, terraced garden to say goodbye to Ted. It suited her very well to find him deep in conversation with a favourite customer for then all that was needed was a cheery wave of the hand and an agreed, 'See you next week.' She guessed he was probably relieved not to be questioned again about the letter – well, communication he called it – from Mum.

As she cycled home Rachel tried again to decide whether to tell her father about Janet's message. Would her mother want him to know? After all, the message was intended for her; if Janet had wished to let her husband know she was all right then surely she'd have written to him instead. All that seemed completely logical to Rachel and she was sure no one would blame her if she remained silent at home. On the other hand, was she being fair to him? And might he be able to think of a way in which they could now discover Janet's whereabouts? Rachel decided to play the whole thing by ear and see what happened when she talked to him.

To her surprise, he was watching television. Normally he took himself off on a Saturday afternoon to see a rugby match or go for a long walk along the cliffs because, he always claimed, he needed 'acres of fresh air after being cooped up over other people's account books all week'. At times both Rachel and her mother had suspected he might be escaping with a friend but he'd been spotted enough times by Shelley or Carly for that theory to be disproved: Roy Blythe was always on his own. It appeared he was one of nature's seekers after solitude.

'Dad, you OK?' she inquired when she became aware he was watching the set with empty eyes, completely ignorant of the fighting taking place in front of him.

'Oh, hello,' he greeted her with a half-smile. Then he sat up straight, pushing his long fingers through his thinning hair in a familiar gesture. 'Where've you been?'

'You know where I've been, where I go every Saturday now. Ted Heywood's. Doing his books and correspondence. Have you been asleep or something? Dad, are you all right?'

He grimaced. 'Bit of a headache, that's all. I've been worrying – thinking – about a work problem. Nothing to bother you with, though.'

She wasn't convinced that was all that was troubling him. But because he so rarely displayed emotion she could never guess what he was thinking or whether anything good or bad had happened to him. Sometimes he picked at a cuticle, the only hint he ever gave that something out of the ordinary might be on his mind.

'There hasn't been a phone call, has there?' she asked, hope suddenly rising. If Mum had written to Ted then might she have phoned her husband?

'Who d'you think might have telephoned?' he asked in a level tone, for once looking straight at her.

'Well, Mum, of course, who else?!' How could he be so insensitive that he hadn't a clue what she meant? Or was he deliberately being obstructive when he must know she needed reassurance?

He produced one of his theatrical sighs and she knew she was going to hear nothing of value. 'It really is time you gave up this feeble idea, Rachel, that your mum is going to telephone us out of the blue. If she hasn't rung by now I think you can take it for granted that she won't ring. She decided to walk out on us and that's it. By now, it's time you accepted it. *I* have. I believe we're in the past as far as she's concerned. Clearly, she's had enough of us.'

'I won't accept it!' Rachel hurled at him, incensed by his indifference to what he saw as their fate. 'I won't! I'm going to find her even if you don't want to. I care about her, even if you don't. I love her – even if you don't.'

That final remark surprised her. She hadn't known she could speak to him as passionately about something so intimate, so vital. She stopped because for the moment she'd said all she could say; but she also needed to observe his reaction.

For a moment or two he didn't respond, his gaze travelling back to the silent screen. Then, mildly as before, he said: 'You seem to know me better than I know myself. You seem to know things about me and your mother that I never realized. How've you managed that?'

Rachel, her temper still rising, told him: 'Because I see with my own eyes what's going on! I see how different we are from any other family I come across. They talk to each other, they laugh and joke, they tell each other things, husbands and wives and children all together. You and Mum never talked, did you? You just had, well, lives. Most of the time we were together it was like being in a morgue.'

That, she was sure, would antagonize him; but it didn't seem to because, still without a change of expression, he replied: 'That's your opinion. But you aren't around all the time. You've no idea what your mother and I talk about, talked about, when we're on our own. Which we were for a lot of every day, you know. We also share a bedroom.'

Rachel chewed the inside of her lip. He had moved the argument into an area where he would have all the answers. But she wasn't going to let him win. 'Well,' she said in a softer tone, 'if you got on so brilliantly with Mum why aren't you out looking for her? Why don't you put everything else out of your mind and go and get her back? If you care so much.'

'I've just repeated to you, Ray, that your mother left of her own free will. I've told you that several times. It was clearly what she wanted, maybe even needed, to do. You simply can't control somebody else's life and I never made any attempt to control hers. That's why *you* have so much freedom, too, remember. I don't lay down lots of ground rules. You're not told to do this or that. Sometimes I think maybe we haven't been strict enough with you but, well, that's not what we're on about at present.'

He paused, shooting a glance at her as if expecting some comment; but when she said nothing he continued in the same mild tone: 'You've also got to remember that I have a living to earn. Somebody has to produce the income that pays for this house and the food we eat and the clothes we wear and the taxes and the electricity and the water and the gas and every other darned thing that costs money. I could add to that list but it would be tedious, wouldn't it? You've got the picture.'

She felt she had been leading by at least two games to love but suddenly the match was level; and, worse, his first serve was going straight in and winning the point. Yet she knew she had truth on her side. 'All right, I know all that, Dad. But there's got to be a reason for Mum's disappearance. If you know so much of what goes on in her mind why don't you know that? If we knew *why* she'd gone we might be able to work out *where* she's gone.'

'Well, you may not have seen it, but there was always, always, a sort of light behind her eyes,' he told her in a strangely reminiscent manner. 'It was as if she had thoughts going on of something else, or someone else, perhaps, thoughts that were lighting up her secret life. I used to wonder sometimes if it could possibly be one of those flower buyers I've never met. But then, I doubt that. The light was there long before she started flogging flowers for a bit of pin money.'

That unexpected revelation galvanized Rachel. 'But if you kept seeing that why didn't you ask her about it? Ask her what was going on in her secret life? I mean, you must have wanted to know.'

Roy Blythe smiled faintly. 'Oh, I did. But it was no good. She would never tell me. I did try, Ray, but Janet just laughed it off. Told me everyone was entitled to some private thoughts. Couldn't disagree, really. You know, I've usually gone along with whatever your mother wanted in life.'

She took a deep breath before she risked her next question. 'Mum once said you married a bit quickly. I didn't realize what that meant then because I was only little. But I know now. You had to get married, didn't you, because I was on the way?'

To her surprise, the question didn't appear to faze, or as she'd half-feared, infuriate him. 'No, we didn't have to. We married because we wanted to. I knew I wanted her to be my wife and so the sooner she was the better.'

'And Mum wanted that, too, not just because of me? Come on, Dad, I think I'm entitled to know. I'm old enough now, old enough to be left on my own, anyway.'

He nodded, as though agreeing with everything she said. 'Yes, she definitely wanted us to marry, she was just as keen as I was. Keener, if anything. And no, before you jump in, not because you were on the way. I believe she was genuinely in love with me. And I believe I was genuinely in love with her.' He paused, hinted at a smile and added: 'There, will that do? Have you heard all you want to hear?'

Rachel frowned. He was taking command of the conversation again. Yet she still had learned nothing of value about the relationship, nothing that might provide a clue as to why Mum had vanished. She got up off the sofa and walked round in a tight circle, thinking furiously about what she could ask next while her father was in this surprisingly communicative mood. Then she remembered something Mum had once casually mentioned. 'Before you got married you hadn't really known each other very long, had you?'

He nodded again. 'That's true. But not important, I think. The important bit is getting to know the person after you've married them, the real person.'

Rachel decided to plunge into deep waters again,

whatever the consequences. 'So what about o
friendships, relationships, that you and Mum h
before you met? I mean, that's something nobody ev
talks about but they must have been important.'

He shook his head vigorously. 'Not important at all.
I never had any *relationships* as you call them – and
your mother, well, I didn't inquire. All that mattered
was how we were with each other. Rachel, I don't think
this inquisition is getting us anywhere. It's certainly
not helping the present situation.'

'But it might be,' she persisted, abruptly sitting
down again opposite him. 'I mean, you said Mum had
a sort of faraway light behind her eyes. Something like
that. Well, maybe it had – has – to do with before you
knew her. Perhaps she's still thinking about an old
boyfriend.'

He shrugged and the half-smile was back. 'Possibly
but highly unlikely, I'd've said. I'm sure I'd've discovered something about that before now. Also, I can't
believe she'd wait fifteen years to catch up on news of
an old flame. It couldn't have been burning in secret
for *that* long!'

His rare attempt at a joke encouraged her to keep
going. 'All right then, so what she was thinking about
doesn't go as far back as that. But you think it started
before she began selling flowers, this secret thinking
about somebody or something. That's what you said.
So, do you think she's gone off to see somebody,
another man I suppose, to sort things out? And that
when it's sorted out she'll come back to us? Is that
what you believe, Dad?'

This time the shake of the head was accompanied by

a spread of the hands. 'I've just no idea, and that's the truth of it, as I keep telling you. One thing seems clear to me, though: she wants time on her own, time maybe to think things out, decide on some course of action or other. I don't mind giving her that, if it's so important to her. We can cope. We're having to, aren't we? But we're surviving.'

His complacency annoyed her. 'But is Mum? Is Mum surviving? We don't know that, Dad, and we ought to.'

His attention was back with the troublesome cuticle. 'I think she'd let us know if anything were wrong. She can pick up a phone anywhere and she knows I'm here. Well, usually here. She knows my routine well enough.'

Once again she jumped to her feet, unable to sit still while that complacency existed. 'But we don't know, that's the point. How do we know she hasn't had a, a breakdown or something? Lost her mind? Gone off without even realizing what she was doing?' She moved agitatedly around the room, looking at nothing, not even at her father until, as if determined on confrontation, she went to stand right in front of him, blocking his view of the TV screen to which his eyes still strayed at intervals. 'That's what we've got to worry about, isn't it, what's happening to *her*?' she demanded.

Her fears didn't move him. 'I don't believe that's possible. Your mother was perfectly rational the last time I talked to her. She didn't have headaches or anything like that. The only problem with her mind is who, or what, it's fixed on: in other words, who or

what, is more important to her at present than you and me. And we can't even begin to guess about that. Well, I know I can't.'

He abandoned his skin-picking operation and glanced up at his daughter. 'Look, she must have planned her departure, you know that. She took a case of clothes and necessities, didn't she? Enough, but not too much. Most of her possessions are still here, still exactly where she left them. She knows they're safe with us. In my view, she left them because she knew she'd be coming back. We don't know when but I think we've just got to be patient.'

Now she glared at him. She wanted to grab and shake him vigorously, shake some urgency, some sense of caring, into him. She wanted to shock him into positive action. She didn't know whether he really felt it was best to do nothing or whether he cared so little that he wasn't prepared to do something. But she couldn't be like that; her feelings for Mum were entirely different, that was obvious. She was going to take some action but it looked as though she'd be on her own. If her dad was willing to write off his wife in such a callous manner then there was nothing to be gained by telling him about Ted Heywood's letter. It might, if she did tell him, be greatly to her disadvantage. Her father might find a way of preventing her doing whatever it was she decided to do. There was one thing, though, she ought to establish, one thing she really needed to be sure about.

'Mum left without any warning, without saying where she was going,' she reminded him. 'How do I know you won't do the same? How do I know I won't

97

get home from school one day and find the house completely deserted? Mum gone – and then you gone?'

She didn't think she'd ever seen him look so startled. 'But that's ridiculous! I've no intention of doing any such thing.'

'Mum might have told me the same thing, but she went,' Rachel continued remorselessly. 'So how can I be sure it won't happen again? I'm not the only one who's had this idea, either.'

'What! What on earth are you talking about now, Ray? Who's said anything like that? Not that dreadful old windbag, Gloria Aries?'

Having sparked fire from him, she sank back on to the sofa. 'No, just somebody at school,' she said evenly. 'Just came out with it. "What would you do if your dad left, too?" Just like that. Really surprised me. I mean, it had never occurred to me. But another girl – a bit of a stirrer – she said, "Well, if one parent pushes off without any warning, why not the other?" I know she wasn't really serious but, well, it made me think.'

'Well, I'm glad the idea was only a bit of schoolgirl banter, or something like that,' he told her, plainly relieved. 'Rachel, you'll just have to take my word for it: I'm not going anywhere. That's definite. And I certainly wouldn't walk out on you in the way your mother did.'

She nodded, finding no difficulty in believing him. Fleetingly she wondered if he ever imagined *she* might be the next one to disappear; after all, she'd told him several times that if her mother didn't return soon she, Rachel, would go and look for her. So far that had been just a cry of despair. Next time she wouldn't waste breath telling him her intentions: she'd go without further delay.

'Look, I need some air, need some exercise, too,' he told her, apparently reassured by her calmness and confident there'd be no more squalls today. 'You've got your own plans for the rest of the day, I take it?'

She nodded again, her mind switching to what she might rustle up for lunch, a meal he often ignored. For all she knew, he might even be going off to a pub for food with a mate, although she didn't think he drank much at any time and she wasn't aware of any friend he ever went out with even on an irregular basis.

Before he was out of the house she was heating up soup and preparing her favourite cereal in a bowl with chopped apples and pineapple chunks. It was, she decided, to be total relaxation from now on for the rest of the day: reading, listening to music, watching a video, chatting to a few friends on the phone if any of them were in and not, like Shelley and her sisters, dutifully visiting grandparents. That was exactly how the day turned out; and so it took her by surprise when she got into bed that she couldn't sleep. Her fears and worries suddenly flooded back and filled her mind.

Her thoughts kept returning to her conversation with her father. Did her parents really have much love for each other? If not then what kept them together (correction: what had kept them together) for so many years? Hard as she tried, she couldn't imagine either of their lives before they met each other, mainly because they had never talked about those times. Once her mother had been the age Rachel was now: so how had she felt then, what were her ambitions? Who were her friends? There must have been at least one boyfriend before she met Dad. People were never as innocent as they sometimes tried to make out. Yet Rachel had no doubt at all that she'd never learn the answers to those questions.

She turned on her left side, wrapping her arms tightly round herself as she'd done when she was quite small and feeling miserable because her parents refused to let her do something she was desperate to do, such as go to tea with an unsuitable (in their eyes) friend or spend all her accumulated pocket money on a plasticky model horse that they said was hideous and she knew was beautiful. It didn't do any good: many minutes later sleep was still eluding her.

'Mum,' she murmured to herself, 'Mum, where are you? Oh, please tell me.' Would her prayers ever be answered? She was beginning to doubt it: as week followed newsless week the doubts were multiplying. If only she knew the reason: that'd be something. A lot, actually. Was it anything to do with herself? Had she in some way so disappointed, so hurt her mother that she was the true cause of Mum's departure? But what could she have done? Nothing: she could think of nothing. But there was a reason, there had to be because Mum wouldn't have gone just for the sake of it. Even her father recognized that, in spite of the fact that he wasn't willing to try to work out real answers to the conundrum.

It would have been easier if her mum had been killed in a car accident or died on the operating table, however terrible that news would have been. At least Rachel would then be sure she wasn't the cause of the disappearance. She'd said something like that to Shelley and Shelley had been horrified by that 'terrible thought', as she described it. But in those circumstances she'd have been spared the present agonizing uncertainty, Rachel added; but, again, there'd been no sympathy or understanding from Shelley whose attitudes to family ranged from despair to devotion. Rachel had once remarked that it must be wonderful to have brothers and sisters – well, just one of either would be better than her own nothing – but Shelley laughed that off and said: 'You should be so lucky! Wish I had my own room and total attention devoted just to me by my ever-loving parents.' Rachel was never sure whether Shelley really meant that; and she suspected that Shelley herself didn't know whether she meant it, either.

On the other hand, Shelley and her siblings each had a high degree of independence, if only because their parents couldn't possibly watch over each of them for most of the time. For her part, Rachel believed that she was too much dependent on her mother; perhaps if she'd fought earlier for a greater degree of independence at home she'd'd've been better able to cope with the present crisis.

'Oh, what's the use,' she groaned aloud, turning over for the hundredth time since getting into bed. 'Oh Mum, where are you? I want you back in my life. I have no one else. Even if Dad doesn't want you any more, I do. *Please* come home. *Please*.'

She thought she might have dozed a little after that for suddenly she realized she was sitting up and saying very solemnly to herself in a low voice: 'But I don't think you are going to come home on your own, are you? Not now, not after so long. So I'm going to come and find you, find you wherever you are. And nobody's going to stop me.'

And, after that, she slept, very soundly.

7

She hadn't expected it to be so dark. At 5.45 a.m. there wasn't a hint of the dawn to come and the widely spaced street lights illuminated best the swirling drizzle. She shivered, and not only because the central heating wasn't on yet, and hoped it would be brighter and drier when she left the house in about forty minutes. In case it wasn't, however, she decided to switch from her usual breakfast to provide what she hoped would be inner warmth.

As she ate she rehearsed her explanation for such an unprecedented early start to her day in case her father also rose earlier than usual. 'I'm doing a trial run for a newspaper delivery round. Don't know if I'll get it but I want to see if I'm up to it – oh, sorry, no pun intended!' A feeble joke like that might divert him from asking any unwelcome questions. In all probability, though, he wouldn't display the slightest interest in her break with routine. If he did want to know more then she would launch into another prepared speech about her need to add to her pocket money. If he heard that he might offer to increase her income himself; at times, he could be fairly generous (in her blacker moments Rachel unkindly supposed that might be her father's way of compensating her for his lack of support in other areas).

However, he still hadn't appeared by the time she wheeled her bike out of the garage and headed at speed for Grimscar Row on the other side of town. As usual, cars were already flowing down Anchor Avenue, a main thoroughfare, in a steady stream but she was soon astonished by how many other people were about: a couple of boys of her own age, doubtless on their way to pick up the newspapers they were to deliver; inevitably, milkmen; dog-walkers of both sexes and a female cat-walker (except that she was holding the sleek Siamese in her arms as if he were too fragile to be allowed on rough ground); and others presumably on their brisk way to bus station or railway station. A man in a trilby and swinging the obligatory businessman's briefcase was in such a good mood that he even called out: 'Good morning!' as if he'd known her personally for years. It was nice to find someone so cheerful at daybreak.

The climb from Pathways, on the rise above the town centre, to Grimscar Row itself was too severe in places for her to be able to ride all the way. It was the part of the journey she always resented on Saturdays but any other route would be so much longer it simply wasn't worth considering.

Now with the drizzle worsening into steady rain, she loathed it all the more, wishing, too, that she'd worn old slacks instead of her short skirt for school. If it went on like this she'd have to return home to change before going on to school; and that would be to risk an unwanted encounter with her father if he hadn't left for work. Maybe this wasn't such a brilliant idea after all. It definitely wouldn't be if she'd miscalculated and there was no second letter from her mother to Ted Heywood. But she *had* to believe it would turn up. She felt at this moment that her life absolutely depended on it.

Instead of leaving her bike in the usual place beside the shed, she carefully hid it behind convenient fruit bushes at the end of the terrace nearer the entrance to what Ted always called The Flower Gardens. As she cautiously made her way along the flagged path to the mail-box she felt like a thief in the night. How on earth would she explain her presence at this time of day if, for some unpredictable reason, Ted himself or anyone else happened to turn up and see her? She'd tried to work out a convincing excuse for such an emergency but the best she'd been able to come up with was that she'd lost a bracelet or keepsake ring the previous Saturday and was certain she must have mislaid it here. It wouldn't take a particularly acute mind or line in questioning to prove how threadbare that story was.

The postman hadn't been yet! That discovery, as she scraped her hand around inside the box, almost unhinged her. Through careful, if seemingly casual, questioning of Ted the previous week she'd established that The Flower Gardens were always one of the postman's first calls on his daily round. 'Bit of a waste, really, as I can never be bothered to look at the stuff until dinner-time, anyway,' Ted pointed out. 'And on Fridays I don't bother at all because I know you'll be here next day to take care of it all. Nothing's as urgent as some folk would like to believe, you know. In this life, there's far too much rush, rush, rush.' Well, on this occasion, she could've done with the postman rushing to work even earlier than usual.

She looked at her watch again, calculating the time she could afford to hang around here to check the post before hurrying away again, first home to change, then to school. If he didn't come soon she might have to think again about the home diversion however wet she got. 'Oh, come on, please come on!' she pleaded – and, at once, remembered how, at night, she kept pleading with her mother to return home. That plea wasn't being answered. So what were her chances with this one?

Then, before that thought was out of her mind, she saw the headlights of a vehicle on the lane leading to The Flower Gardens. She hadn't any doubt who it was and, sure enough, moments later the driver was out of his van, leaving the engine running, and striding towards the mail-box, several letters in his hand. Rachel, crouching behind the low stone wall beside The Shed, watched him, nerves jangling and hardly daring to breathe. Of course, he couldn't possibly hear her, she knew that; but she couldn't help trying to hold her breath. Again she was swept by fears that she was acting like a criminal and shortly would be indulging in criminal activity. But nothing, now, was going to prevent her from doing what she'd come to do.

Waiting until the postman was back in his van and reversing and then heading back down the lane, she hurried to the mail-box and took out everything that had just been put in. By now there was almost enough daylight to read by but she still used the torch, shading it so that the beam fell only on to the address on each envelope.

They were mostly familiar to her: bills from suppliers, payments from customers, invitations to invest or subscribe to this or that and then, the only surprise, a postcard from someone called Lizzie who was having a 'lovely little break with Sarah in Oxford'.

She sighed with disappointment and returned the mail to the box. Some of it, without doubt, she'd see again on Saturday morning when she turned up to do Ted's paperwork. It had been a long shot and it hadn't come off. But then, she hadn't expected to be lucky the first time she came to check on Ted's post. That would have been like backing a hundred-to-one winner and even the Grand National didn't turn up many winners at those odds.

Now that it was daylight she needed to be careful not to be spotted by some nosy person in Grimscar Row. Ted himself might turn up at any time and he, above all, was best avoided. The rain had slackened again by the time she reached the town centre but she felt it would be best to go home and change. If she didn't then the sharp-eyed Shelley would be sure to make some comment about the state of her clothing; and, with her, carefully structured lies were always undesirable.

'Something wrong?' her father inquired as she quite literally bumped into him in the entrance hall. He was on the point of leaving for work and doing a final check on his briefcase.

'Not really, just went out for some fresh air and got

107

a bit wet,' she told him as nonchalantly as possible. 'Has the post arrived yet?'

He gave her a second surprised look. 'Of course not. You know we never get a delivery as early as this. Are you expecting something important?'

'Only the usual, something from Mum,' she replied, starting up the stairs. She knew he would make no response to that and she was right. He left without another word.

On each of the remaining weekdays she followed the same routine; and each day came away from her post-box pilgrimage with a sense of desolation. She knew she was setting her hopes far too high but could think of no other way of getting information about her mother's whereabouts. Even if she succeeded in intercepting a message to Mr Heywood there was no guarantee that it would provide a single clue that would help her get closer to Mum. The whole complicated clandestine sequence of getting away from the house and examining Ted's post-box without arousing anyone's suspicions for a single moment was probably a total waste of time and effort. Rachel knew that. But she continued with it because she couldn't think of anything else that would be worth pursuing.

One morning she awoke later than she needed to, the result of an exasperating evening's baby-sitting. She didn't even know the child, a boy who lived further along Anchor Avenue, and she accepted the job only because she hadn't any homework and the money would be useful for when she went to meet her mother. He turned out to be a tyrant and her entire evening in his parents' absence was spent trying to control him until, mercifully, he fell asleep from sheer exhaustion (a state she, too, was approaching rapidly at that point). His favourite trick was to throw all his clothes off and dash away to whatever hiding place he could find; and she daren't leave him to his own devices in case he sneaked out of doors. So, after catching him and stuffing him back into pyjamas and hoping he'd fall asleep *this* time, she couldn't read or watch TV for long before he reappeared and started the sequence again. As she had hardly any experience of boys of any age she wondered whether they were all like this at Craig's age, rude and thoroughly ruthless little show-offs.

She also found herself wondering how her mother would have dealt with someone like Craig. As Rachel was her only child presumably her mum might not have known how to handle him, although, of course, she could call on her experience of dealing with at least one man, Rachel's dad, in her life. Would her mum have left home if she'd had another child, a son? Would a bigger family really have made any difference to Janet Blythe's lifestyle or ambitions, whatever they were? Rachel had no way of answering any of the questions so she abandoned them.

In spite of getting to Grimscar Row later than usual she went through her routine for she'd convinced herself that if she missed a day that would be when the letter arrived – and thus she'd have no chance of reading it for herself. But she was wrong: the mail-box was as unrewarding as on previous days. On the Saturday she approached The Shed with some trepidation for, unusually, Ted was there ahead of her, sitting in the only chair, looking intently at the sheet of paper in his hands. Her heart leapt: had her mother's latest letter arrived by some form of special delivery or had he emptied the mail-box himself and found it there? Was he, this time, going to share it with her?

'Morning, my dear,' he greeted her in his normal tone. Then he gave her an unexpectedly sharp look. 'Been a good week for you, has it?'

'Er, yes, of course, Mr Heywood,' she told him, puzzled as well as marginally alarmed by his manner. Had he heard something about her early morning visits after all? Had she been spotted by someone who passed on suspicions? Was he hoping she would admit her unforgivable behaviour before he sacked her from her part-time job?

He grinned. 'Good, good. You see, I'd like you to do a bit more work for me today, if you wouldn't mind. But I thought, well, if you've had a really hard time at school you'll not be wanting to do extra for me.'

'Oh, anything, anything,' she gushed in relief. 'Honestly, it's just been, well, normal!' She mentally crossed fingers that he wouldn't detect the lie.

'Glad to hear it, my dear. You see, I was just not at my best for a couple of days: nothing to worry about, rheumaticky, really, and my pantry's got a bit low because I've not felt up to replenishing it. So could you just nip off to the shop for a few necessary groceries? I'll pay you for your time, naturally, just like for any other job you do.'

'Of course, Mr Heywood, of course!'

So he dictated a little list, not having presumed on her cooperation by writing one in advance, and she sped off to get what he needed. She added a chocolate bar from her own money almost as a conscience-gesture for she knew he'd not buy it for himself in spite of his admitted liking for sweets. And after that, she did what she usually did, dealt with the mail and the account books and several minor chores. The following Monday she was back at Grimscar Row in her surreptitious role.

On the eighth day she found what she had desperately been looking for.

As she held the envelope addressed in Mum's familiar neat, upright style in the royal blue ink of a pen Rachel had given her as a birthday present her hands began to shake. Momentarily, it was hard to believe that, almost literally, she was in touch again with Mum. To give herself time to think what to do next she carefully replaced the rest of the mail in the box. Should she take the letter away or open and read it here, now? Whatever she did, she'd be committing some sort of criminal act, stealing or interfering with Her Majesty's Mail or whatever the official charge might be. But then, if Ted didn't know the letter had arrived he couldn't complain to anyone that it had been stolen, even supposing he'd want to complain. After all, Rachel had reasoned from the moment she decided to check on his mail-box, if the message it contained was really intended for her ears anyway she was hardly doing anything wrong at all.

She slipped the letter into the inside pocket of her blazer. Even if the light had been better it was too risky to read it now, out in the open, when anyone might spot her if they came along the lane. It was firmly sealed so there was no hope of gently lifting the flap and then later re-sealing it when she'd read the contents. So she'd have to stick to her original plan to substitute another envelope when she returned the letter to Ted's mail-box. It wouldn't be hard to forge a likeness of her mother's handwriting, particularly as Ted was not the sort of man to scrutinize envelopes.

Her face, she was sure, must betray her emotions so she was thankful she encountered no one at all as she hurtled away from Grimscar Row. She'd already selected her spot to read the letter: an isolated shelter on the Promenade. If anyone saw her they'd probably suspect she was reading a letter from a boyfriend (and because that would be more obvious still if the reading were on school premises she definitely had to be elsewhere: Shelley or Carly or another friend would demand to know his identity and not let up until she gave in). She skidded to a halt and rested the bike against the far wall. As she'd known it would be, the ancient, green-painted shelter was deserted at this hour of the day.

She slid her nail under the flap of the ordinary white envelope and somehow managed to do very little damage to it as she pulled it free. The letter consisted of a single sheet, folded once.

Dear Mr Heywood,
I hope you are well and that your rheumatics haven't been bothering you in all the rain recently. I keep thinking of you and hope you didn't mind my asking you to pass on the message to Rachel.

As I expect you can understand, I miss her terribly. Perhaps she even misses me! So I'd be really grateful if you could let her know I'm fine, that I miss her and I send her all my love. She mustn't worry about anything. I will be back, I promise, but I still can't say when. Please ask her to be very, very patient. I haven't gone out of her life for ever. But I'm sure she knows that, really.

I hope everything in the gardens is doing well and that you're still keeping all your customers happy. I'll be in touch again when I can.

Best wishes, Janet Blythe

She let out the breath she'd been holding without realizing it: so it was true! Her Mum did care, after all. That was the most important thing of all to Rachel for it meant she hadn't been abandoned as in her nightmares she'd feared.

Mum was coming back! She'd said so. But, on the downside, there was the ominous plea to be 'very, very patient'. That could only be interpreted in one way: Mum would not be home yet, might not be coming back for weeks and weeks, even . . . years? Well, that had to be a possibility.

Rachel read the letter a second and then a third time, slowly, absorbing each word, looking for something else that might bring comfort. So she was missed – but not, she would bet, half as much as she missed Mum. Idly now, she turned the paper over, just in case there was a meaningful scribble on the other side of the sheet of plain yellow paper. Nothing. She returned to the letter – and then her eye caught the two words at the top of the sheet: Barossa Square.

However could she have missed them! An address – well, an address of some sort. Unless it was deliberately intended to mislead the reader. But why on earth would her mother do that? She'd apparently asked Ted not to show anyone her first letter and she knew he was a person she could trust. She'd expect him to be just as discreet about the next letter, this one, so there was no need to put a false address.

Her heart racing again, Rachel grabbed the envelope to see the franking. How could she have ignored that in the first place? And there it was, plain as could be, London N1.

London, that's where Mum was, London! At last. At last she'd found her. Then she faced reality. Was that her real address in London or had Mum simply posted it there? If only she'd been allowed to see the first letter she'd know whether that, too, bore the same address and postmark. Of course, there was no way she could tell Ted a second letter had arrived and she'd opened it. Out of loyalty to Mum he'd already refused to tell her anything more about that first message.

If she didn't move now she was going to be late for school. Hastily, she stuffed the letter back into its envelope and then into her pocket. Her mind was whirling with thoughts of how she'd locate Barossa Square in London N1. The public library would be the best bet: they'd surely have London guides. There'd be no problem about going round there at the end of the afternoon, though she might have to make some clever excuses to escape Shelley's company.

Already she'd made one decision that nothing would persuade her to revoke: she was going to London to find Mum. If she told no one in advance then no one could stop her. She'd go just as soon as she knew the location of Barossa Square. She'd go and she wouldn't return until she'd found her.

Janet bit her lip and tried to think of another excuse as Melody's request turned into a desperate plea. She wished fervently she'd never telphoned her in the first place for, really, it had been an unnecessary call.

'Janet, you'd be saving my life, you truly would. There's just nobody else in this world I could ask, as if I would, anyway. You know Sebastian adores you, thinks you're almost better than his own mum!'

The tinkling laugh down the line sounded completely genuine. But Janet was not fooled. She knew only too well that Melody would never put herself in second place to anyone. Of course, she couldn't say that, not even hint it, but she had to say something so positive Melody would accept defeat and find another babysitter for tomorrow night.

'Listen, Melody – ' she started to say, only to be drowned by the next deluge.

'Do it for me, Janet, do it for *me*! I'm desperate. Look, I'll pay double the usual rate. That's how much I need you, Janet. Don't say no, Janet!'

It was bewildering because Janet couldn't help wondering what Melody would've done if she, Janet, hadn't telephoned to ask whether she could change her agreed hours slightly the next day. But then, perhaps Melody was expecting to ask her about the extra time when she arrived home from work tomorrow evening; or she could have phoned during the day.

'Melody, I'm really, really sorry but it's just impossible,' Janet said, recognizing that she was almost imitating Melody's own emotive style. 'I've got this meeting and I simply can't miss it, not for anything. I have to see someone very, very special.'

There was, for the first time, a fractional pause as Melody took in the implications of that statement. 'It's a man, then, a man you're dating? Hey, I wondered how long it'd be before you found yourself someone, Janet. I just hope – '

'No, no, it's nothing like that,' Janet replied firmly. 'Definitely not. This is, well, someone completely different. Much more important. But I can't tell you any more. Even my family don't know about it – you know, back home.'

It was plain Melody didn't believe her, but suddenly she surrendered after all. 'Well, OK, Janet, if that's what you want. I'm just so sorry you can't help – and Sebastian will be really down when it's not you looking after him again.'

Janet wondered whether she was expected to read into that statement that Melody might not be wanting her services in the future. But even that threat didn't matter: for if everything went perfectly at tomorrow night's meeting then she wouldn't have to babysit again to earn vital money.

'Sorry again I can't help, Melody,' she said as cheerfully as she could manage. 'I'm sure you'll get someone Sebastian will like. See you tomorrow, then. Bye.'

She hung up, stepped out of the kiosk with a sense of relief and walked briskly away from Barossa Square.

8

The crush astonished her. Although she'd seen pictures of London Underground stations on TV they'd never seemed as crowded as this. You really couldn't move half a metre without having to avoid people. Where, Rachel wondered, were they all going at this time of day? Surely they should have started work before now?

She kept to the back of the platform, up against the tiled wall that began to arch over not so very far above her head, obscuring yet another poster for London's newest film, posters that no one seemed to look at except with blank eyes. 'One minute', the indicator board warned: one minute before she caught the train that would deliver her to Barossa Park Station. One short ride to the end of her journey. The end of the search.

It arrived, as they all did, with a rush. She wasn't opposite one of the sliding doors and when she got to the opening it was jammed with bodies. Even if she'd possessed extra strength and determination she simply couldn't have forced her way into that carriage: for no one looked at her and therefore no one moved aside to help her. Momentarily, she dithered, then turned and dashed down the platform to the next doorway, which was equally packed with people. And before she could try to squeeze in among them the doors began remorselessly to slide across.

Rachel had hopelessly failed to catch the first tube train she'd ever tried to board. 'You idiot!' she railed at herself. 'You're too feeble to catch a cold. Get a grip on yourself, girl!'

She looked round to see who was watching her incompetence, who was smirking or even laughing outright. There were still almost a dozen people there, apparently uninterested in catching the train she missed or perhaps waiting for the next, expecting it to be less crowded. They were all self-absorbed – except for one cigarette-thin girl of perhaps her own age. And she was staring avidly at Rachel as if desperate to know everything about her. Startled, half-embarrassed, Rachel turned away to look up at the flickering indicator board that was now playing some sort of private game with 'next train one minute' chasing and replacing 'next train four minutes'.

'You going somewhere special, then?'

Rachel swung round again to find the girl beside her, looking up intently into her face. How had she managed to move so fast, so silently?

'Er, yes,' she answered automatically, politely.

'Where's that, then?'

The voice was thin but penetrating as a pointed knife. Rachel hesitated this time, instead looking hard at the pale face framed by dense strands of dark brown, curly hair. The eyes were dark, unblinking, focused on her own, unnervingly.

'Barossa Park,' she said, immediately wondering why she was giving information away to a total stranger.

'Same here,' said the girl, with a speed that made Rachel suspicious. What did she want? What was she after? Had it been a man who'd approached her, she wouldn't have replied with so much as a single word. Would she?

Her intelligence snapped back. 'But why didn't you catch the last train, the one I missed?'

'Not in a hurry, am I?' was the answer. Her hands were thrust deep into the side pockets of a worn leather jacket she was wearing over a russet-coloured, round-necked sweater and new-looking blue cord trousers.

Rachel glanced up at the indicator board, trying to decide how to detach herself from this situation. There was nothing she wanted to talk about to this girl, whoever she was and whatever she wanted. Because she must want something.

'Going to see someone, are you, up around Barossa Park?' was the next inquiry.

Rachel took a deep breath. 'Yes. Someone very special. That's who I'm looking for – I mean, going to see. Now – '

'Aren't we all?' came the laconic response; but this time there was a hint of a smile around the neat mouth. Rachel couldn't help seeing that she appeared to have remarkably white and even teeth.

'Listen, why are you asking me these questions? What d'you want?' Rachel was no longer in the mood to surrender the initiative. With a bit of luck, the girl would give up and move off before the next train arrived. Not for a moment did Rachel believe her claim that she, too, was travelling to Barossa Park.

'You look good, don't you?'

The comment was so unexpected it disarmed her completely. No other girl she'd ever known would say something like that to a complete stranger as a conversational gambit or for any other reason. Rachel didn't have any doubt that this girl meant what she said.

'Look, who are you? What's your name?' she asked in a less aggressive manner.

'El, OK.'

Rachel couldn't have heard right, she was sure. 'L? You mean, the letter L, short for something?'

The girl shook her head, curtains of hair swinging across her face from side to side. 'Just El. Don't worry about it.'

The suppressed roar of the approaching train hardly distracted Rachel at all for the moment. She was floundering over what to ask next but she had to know more. What it was about El that intrigued her she couldn't have told, but there was something.

This time a door opened directly in front of them and this time, too, there was no log jam of bodies to keep Rachel on the platform. El stepped ahead of her on to the train and made for a vacant seat. Without hesitation, Rachel followed her and was able to sit beside her.

'You're on your own, aren't you? Right?' El resumed.

'How – how d'you know that?' answered Rachel instead of instantly denying it.

'I can just tell. It's easy. I just know.'

Rachel tried to recover lost ground. 'I told you, I'm going to see somebody, someone special, so I won't be on my own then. We'll be going home together.'

'Where's that?'

'Rocksea – in the north, you know. By the sea, of course. Look, what about you, where do you live? Are you bunking off school today? I mean, what're you going to do at Barossa Square – sorry, Barossa Park?'

The response was a shrug and for the first time a failure to make direct eye contact. In a low voice El, looking away, said: 'Nowhere, really. Anywhere I find that'll do.'

Astonished by this casualness Rachel tried again. 'Oh, come on. You must live somewhere. Everybody does. Even if it's, well, a cardboard box under a bridge!'

Part of her wanted to avoid this strange girl altogether, as if she were a threat to Rachel's own structured existence, or what used to be structured until Mum disappeared; her other self wanted to know more about someone apparently so totally different from herself.

Another shrug. 'No, that's how it is with me. I like – freedom. Doing what I want, being with who I want.'

'But school . . .'

'School's dead. Cut it out of my life months ago. Waste of time. No freedom there.'

'But – '

'You should do the same. It's easy once you know what you really want.' Now El was staring at her with a fierceness of concentration that Rachel found utterly unsettling; yet she couldn't look away now from El's dark, almost black, gaze. 'Listen, we could share loads of things, you and I. I can help you, I know I can. I think you'll need me.'

It was turning into the most amazing encounter of Rachel's life. Even if she wanted to she sensed she was powerless to escape from it. Then El reached across and took Rachel's thumb and forefinger in her own right hand, her grip surprisingly cool and reassuring.

'Gotta go now,' she declared. 'Gotta get off here.'

As if from a distance Rachel realized the train was slowing down, that other people were getting to their feet. 'But you said – you said you were going to Barossa Park. This can't be it!'

'Going there later on.' El, too, was rising. 'Listen, I'll see you there at 8 o'clock. Top of the steps out of the tube. I'll be there, I swear it. See you then. I'll be your friend, remember that.'

Without a backward glance she was off, shoulders hunched, spearing between slower passengers as if desperate to get away or catch another train that wouldn't wait. Rachel felt dazed. The suddenness of the departure was perhaps the most astounding thing of all about the few minutes she'd spent with El. Ten minutes ago – no more – she'd known nothing of the girl's existence; now, because she'd gone, she felt bereft.

Why, why, why had she chosen Rachel to talk to like that? What did she really want? Who is she? Rachel couldn't even start to think constructively about possible answers to those immediate questions. Until El first spoke to her all she could think about was the search for her mother and her journey all that morning from Rocksea via York and King's Cross and crowds everywhere. It would never have occurred to her to speak to anyone she didn't know unless it was for information or help. She couldn't imagine ever seeking to befriend a stranger in such a direct way. It was one of the things she admired already about El. What on earth could that name stand for?

When, five stations further on, the train reached Barossa Park station, Rachel gave up trying to make sense of meeting El (who, she remembered with another rush of astonishment, hadn't even asked Rachel her name). Yet, as she slowly climbed the steps into daylight she was thinking of her again because this must be where El would be at 8 o'clock, waiting for her. Why was she so certain that Rachel would want to meet her again? Impossible to answer.

To get to the square itself she had to walk from the station entrance along a narrow street of newer, featureless buildings called, she knew from her library map reading, Barossa Gardens. She moved slowly, wondering how close at this moment she was to her mother. Could she, even at this moment, be coming round the corner? Could a miracle happen and they'd literally bump into each other? What would Mum say when she realized her only daughter had been clever enough to track her down with scarcely a clue to help her?

The square lived up to its name: four sides, all built up, of almost equal length with roads emerging at each corner; and, in the middle, a railed garden with bedraggled bushes and stunted plane trees and dusty paths and a dilapidated shed that might once have been someone's cherished summerhouse. Still moving at snail's pace, she circumnavigated the entire square, gazing up at first and second floor windows, and soon lost count of the number of columns of bell-pushes. Every house appeared to be flatted and every house had at least four floors and most possessed an occupied basement as well. How could she possibly check on every residence to find one person? And yet what else could she do? There were name tags against each bell so, unless Mum had tried to change her identity, she ought to be there under her own name. Rachel tried to dismiss the idea that Mum was already living with somebody else but it remained one of the most formidable of all the obstacles still facing her.

Suddenly, the prospect of checking on every flat overwhelmed her: she needed a drink and something to eat first. Apart from sandwiches on the train she'd eaten nothing since leaving home without bothering with breakfast. She hadn't wanted to alert her father by rattling dishes or even boiling a kettle. In any case, it had been enough of a problem to get to the station in time for her train. She'd left him a note:

Gone to look for Mum. I think I know where she is. Love, R.

For the first hour she kept wondering how he'd react to it. Would he just sigh and push it to one side, or would he this time immediately ring the police to report that his daughter was missing and might be in danger? She decided that was unlikely but then Dad didn't always behave predictably. When she found Mum – and she kept telling herself she *would* find her today – then she'd ring home with the news. This time he wouldn't be left in the dark.

Because she daren't risk going into a pub, although probably no one would challenge her if she did, she needed a snack bar. There was nothing of that kind in the square, only, on one adjoining corner, a mini-supermarket with sleeves of advertising cards in a couple of windows. It was called All Hours, doubtless because that was when it was open: rather neat, she thought. It would have to suffice if she could find nothing else but really she wanted something hot before she started on the slog of knocking on doors (or, rather, ringing bells and talking into security systems built into door posts). In an alleyway that slanted off a side street she found what she was looking for and was surprised by the hygienic gleam of the glass-fronted counter and plastic table tops.

'Yes, Miss, what can I get you?' a man in a white chef's outfit greeted her. 'Here everything is the best you'll find anywhere.'

She returned his grin as she studied the chalked temptations on the blackboard above his head. Every-one at school seemed to agree that nobody in London would ever say a kind word to anyone else. All they thought about was getting every penny they could out of you. 'Pizza is freshly made, Miss, just perfect for taste and energy.' He sounded as if he meant every word and she surrendered. She couldn't remember the last time she'd had a pizza in the middle of the day – her school never offered anything so original – but suddenly it was exactly what she wanted.

It turned out to be just as good as the proprietor's promise. Because the snack bar, or ristorante as she saw it was called, was almost empty she couldn't ignore his beaming pleasure when he saw how rapidly she ate; so, self-consciously, she signalled her approval by toasting him with her glass of Coke, a gesture she'd never have thought of let alone tried out in Rocksea. She let him persuade her to have a coconut slice and a large cup of cappuccino. Then she thought of Shelley and immediately began to miss her. Normally when she ate out it was with Shelley – her parents never thought of going out for a meal just for the sake of it as other families might – and today there'd've been so much to talk about. As it was, she hadn't said a word to her best friend about her trip to London. Shelley, she feared, would have found it impossible not to disclose the news to somebody: and if that somebody had been a teacher then her plans would have been in jeopardy or, worse, the school would have warned the London police who then might have started to search for her. All the same, she wished Shelley were with her now so they could share the laborious business of checking out the occupants of the houses and flats in Barossa Square. It was the sort of thing Shelley might relish.

'Please come back, we like to have smart young people in our restaurant,' the chef told her with continuing gallantry as she paid her bill and politely confirmed how much she'd enjoyed the food. She felt herself colouring slightly at this second compliment to her appearance within an hour or so. She was wearing her favourite black jacket and red silk blouse because she needed to feel good; and to show Mum her standards hadn't declined in her absence. A stranger or a snack bar owner in Rocksea would never have made personal remarks like that, she was sure. Yet the boost to her ego was a real bonus. At least it would improve her confidence when people answered her ring at their doorbell.

In fact, no one at all responded to any of the first five bells she rang and supplementary rat-tat-tats on the doors themselves were equally fruitless. 'Surely not everybody's out!' she told herself. Of course, none of the names beside the bell pushes was 'Blythe' or anything like it but she'd decided it wouldn't be a waste of time to ask a resident if they knew of her mother or recognized her from the photo Rachel was ready to display. It wasn't very recent because her parents didn't care for being photographed and Rachel had never been given a camera. The snap was one Shelley had taken during a summer picnic in their garden; even at the time it had seemed shameful to Rachel that the picnic site was their familiar garden instead of on the cliffs or the beach or somewhere normal people went for such an outing. Janet Blythe had been in a good mood that afternoon and for once she hadn't objected to being snapped. Perhaps, Rachel later reflected, Mum had supposed that Shelley's skills with her new camera were so limited the picture wouldn't come out. Almost as if anticipating that one day she'd really need that full-face picture, Rachel kept it hidden among her private treasures.

'Oh, come on!' she urged as she tried a bell marked

Metlinski for the third time. And suddenly the door swung open and a small man in a red cardigan with a deeply lined face confronted her.

'What you want?' he demanded.

She smiled as sweetly as she knew how. 'I wondered if you know somebody called Mrs Blythe. She lives in the square but I'm not sure of the number. Could you help, please?'

'Who you – police? No, too young. Snooper. You snooper?'

The tone was getting fiercer by the word and Rachel was taken aback by the antagonism.

'No, no,' she protested, still trying to smile. 'It's my mum I'm looking for – look, this is her picture. Have you seen her?'

'Go away,' the man ordered, not even deigning to glance at the photograph Rachel held up in front of him. 'You snooping. Me, I don't tell nothing to nobody. Go away or I summon police.'

'But – '

The door slammed in her face and she heard bolts being shot home and a chain rattle. That was the worst experience on the first side of the square but nothing else that happened was exactly encouraging. Most people who answered through security voice boxes assumed immediately she was selling something or collecting for a charity and refused to discuss anything at all with her in spite of Rachel's insistence she wasn't seeking money for herself or anyone else.

At one door she'd just about given up when she heard a key being turned and an elderly but very smartly dressed lady confronted her. She listened to

Rachel's by now well practised patter but scarcely glanced at the proffered photo.

'My dear, you do realize what a dangerous thing you're doing, don't you?' she inquired in cultivated tones.

'Er, well, not really,' Rachel replied truthfully. She knew there might be risks in contacting strangers on their own territory but she'd already decided that the one thing she wouldn't do was accept any invitation to enter a house.

The woman, hand stroking the pearls at her throat, shook her head as if unable to credit such naïvety. 'My dear, the world is full of wicked people, people who would certainly take advantage of your youth and loveliness. You must be constantly on your guard against villainy. It is most unwise to put yourself in a vulnerable position like this. You must take care. Is there no one with you?'

'Not at the moment,' said Rachel, wishing she didn't sound so feeble. 'But I know how to take care of myself, thanks. I'm always prepared for any, er, problems.'

'I sincerely hope so,' the woman said in a tone that lacked conviction. 'Goodbye to you then, and take care.'

Within five minutes of that experience Rachel was wondering if the woman had been giving her a deliberate warning about the man who answered the bell only a few doors away. Middle-aged, he was barefoot and dressed in pyjamas and Rachel's first thought was to apologize for getting him out of bed. As she started to speak, he stepped forward, glanced around in furtive fashion and then pulled open the front of his trousers. Hastily Rachel backed away but couldn't help seeing what he wanted her to see. She didn't glance back when she reached the bottom of the steps but she heard the slam of the door.

Sickened, she looked round for somewhere to rest for a few minutes. In spite of what had just happened she knew she'd doggedly continue with her task of asking anyone she could find for help. The central garden, she saw, had an entrance that was open and she went across to it, choosing a seat beside some dusty bushes that might screen her from passers-by. She knew she might be even more at risk in such a spot but her fingers closed round the whistle she'd armed herself with before leaving home. She had no idea whether it would afford any protection but it was better than nothing. If she were approached by someone intent on harming her then the whistle just might scare him off; at the very least it would alert anyone within hearing distance that someone needed help.

She didn't want to think about the man in the pyjamas but she remembered now he hadn't spoken a single word. That alone should have warned her he was up to no good. Perhaps he always dressed like that, just waiting for any female to come to his door. Oh, if only she could talk to Shelley or any other sane, intelligent, caring person! But her watch told her Shelley wouldn't be home from school yet and, even, if she were, it was an expensive time of the day to telephone. How much time would she get for £1? Yet she'd have to ring, she'd go mad if she couldn't make contact with a friend. No one came into the garden and, for a few minutes, she felt able to resume her inquiries. Oh Mum, you must be somewhere close by. Please, please come to the door and agree we can go home together today. Rachel closed her eyes and crossed her fingers and prayed again to whoever could arrange these things for her. Neither she nor her parents had ever believed in God, any God, and it seemed to her that everything that happened in life proved she was right to ignore religious beliefs.

The third side of the square proved to be better populated than the previous two sides: or, as she decided, more people were prepared to answer the bell or door-knocker. Even so, there was no reward at all until a young woman in black jeans and scarlet sweater greeted her with a quick smile and a very businesslike manner.

'Look, I'm sorry to bother you,' Rachel apologized immediately, trying a new approach. She held up the photograph. 'This is my mum and I'm desperate to find her. Do you happen to have seen her round here?'

The woman took the photo, examined it closely and then nodded briskly. 'Yes, I'm sure I have seen her quite a few times.'

Rachel's heart leapt. After so many disappointments she could hardly believe what she was hearing. 'Honestly? I mean, you really have seen her?'

The woman's smile was warmer now and lasted longer. 'I'm a fashion designer – yes, I know I'm dressed casually now but that's because I'm not working today. So, you see, I'm used to observing people, women especially, and noting what they're wearing, whether it's suitable. I've seen this woman in a red-

and-blue floral pleated skirt and powder blue blouse, I remember. Would that be an outfit of hers?'

'Oh yes, definitely. I was actually with her when she bought that skirt in York on a day out.' Rachel was so excited she wanted to tell this woman every single thing about herself and about Mum's disappearance. But that was stupid. She must remain calm. 'Can you tell me where she's living then?'

The smile vanished and Rachel's hopes plummeted. 'Sorry, I can't, but I should think it must be somewhere in the vicinity. I've seen her crossing the road by the shop over there and once I definitely saw her *in* the shop. One evening, it was. You may have seen, it's called All Hours and that really is when it's open.'

Rachel's eyes were glowing. 'Oh, thank you. You're the first person to have spotted her. Honestly. I can't tell you how grateful I am.'

'Good, good.' The dark-haired woman seemed genuinely pleased to have been of help. Her hand went up to one of her gold ear-rings, shaped like camels, that looked as if they'd cost the earth. 'Look, I'd invite you in, see if I can remember anything else, though I don't suppose I can, except I'm going out in a few minutes. You only just caught me.'

'No, no, that's all right. Honestly, I'm so grateful. But do you think she is living in Barossa Square? I mean, do you know any neighbours who might have seen her and know her actual address?'

The shrug and the grimace of disappointment said everything. 'Sorry, I know hardly anybody personally. People round here just seem to keep themselves to themselves in my experience. I expect somebody knows something but I truly can't suggest anyone. Unless, well, I suppose you could try the shop. Mr Dalal, he's Indian and the owner. I think he's your best bet. Sorry, but I must dash. But good luck with your search.'

'Thanks a lot, I'm really grateful,' Rachel managed to say before, with a flashing smile, the young woman closed the door. She wished they'd been able to talk longer. But, at least, she'd been a great help and Rachel's spirits were still rising.

Now she was torn between continuing her house-to-house inquiries and going across to the shop. But the shop had to come first because Mum had actually been seen in there. Quite possibly, she was a regular customer; she was almost bound to be if she lived in the neighbourhood. Maybe Mr Dalal knew her well.

But, on this day of all days, Mr Dalal wasn't there. 'Sorry,' said the lank-haired girl at the check-out and sounding nothing of the sort. 'Can't help you. Mr Dalal has had to go to see his brother who has been taken ill. I'm only filling in for him, I don't normally work here. So I can tell you nothing about this woman you are seeking.'

'But isn't there anyone else who works here regularly?' Rachel persisted. She couldn't bear having her hopes dashed yet again after such a breakthrough. 'I mean, Mr Dalal isn't the only person who'd know the customers, is he?'

Solemn-faced, the girl shook her head. 'Mr Dalal is always here on his own or with his brother, except today, of course. You will have to come back another time if you wish to ask him your questions. I am sorry I cannot help you.'

She turned then to attend to a patient customer. Rachel, reluctant to leave without gaining something from the visit, wandered down the aisle of canned goods. It seemed to her just like any other mini-supermarket, apart from the rather exotic-sounding packages that were probably provided for customers of widely differing ethnic backgrounds. There was also a larger selection of honeys than she'd seen elsewhere and, uniquely in her experience, a section devoted to fairly pricey stationery. Did the inhabitants of Barossa Square and the neighbouring streets spend a lot of their free time writing letters? Probably several of them had families overseas, so that might account for it. Janet Blythe had also written letters from here: so was this where she bought her stationery? Somehow, that thought raised her hopes again.

'Look, can you give me any idea at all when Mr Dalal might be back? I really do need to talk to him,' Rachel asked anxiously when she could claim the girl's attention again. 'I mean, this is really, really important.'

'I am sorry I cannot help you,' was the polite but totally impersonal reply. 'I don't know when Mr Dalal will return. But I am sure he will be back as soon as possible. He does not like ever to be away from his store. So, tomorrow, perhaps.'

Rachel nodded. 'OK, thanks. I'll be here as soon as I can and hope to see him.'

She edged past the sleeves of advertisements in order to allow another customer to reach the check-out and left the shop with a sense of renewed gloom. Just when she seemed to be making progress and had something to look forward to she immediately suffered a setback. It was like snakes-and-ladders. At present, the snakes were definitely defeating her. What to do next? She couldn't make up her mind. The thought of knocking on more doors and risking encounters with sick monsters or paranoid pensioners was just too depressing. It was too early to return to the ristorante, even though she fancied the idea of a long slow drink of coffee; and, in any case, the proprietor would probably still be there, eager to ask *her* lots of questions. She had an idea that, if she wanted it, she could easily get him to offer her a job as a waitress or cashier or something like that.

By now she knew she'd have to stay in London overnight. Her original best hope was that she'd find Mum soon after reaching Barossa Square and then, after a good sorting out of all that had been happening, they'd return home to Rocksea together in triumph. At worst she'd supposed it would take a couple of days to track her down and so she'd taken enough money to pay for a night in a decent small hotel as well as for meals and travel on buses and the tube. Before leaving home she'd checked out hotel prices with a travel agent and discovered she could easily afford quality bed-and-breakfast accommodation. She'd pondered what to do about her father. The message she'd left for him might be enough to assuage fears he might have about her safety, though she couldn't even be sure he'd worry about that anyway. As he hadn't wanted to go in pursuit of his wife he was hardly likely to show greater concern about Rachel's whereabouts, especially as she'd explained what she was up to. So, no, she really didn't have to worry about what he would do; because Roy Blythe would almost certainly do nothing at all.

Rachel looked at her watch again. Oh, to hell with the expense: she'd ring Shelley *now*. She didn't have to stay on the phone very long for she could always say she was running out of money. She'd spotted a familiar glass coffin, as some of her friends described the latest design, and now she punched in the memorized number. Miraculously, it was Shelley who answered.

'Ray! Where are you? Hey, you've caused a sensation at school. Miss Akehurst couldn't believe you were missing. Said you'd promised to hand in that tourist survey you were supposed to be doing for her. Old Akey couldn't believe you would let her down.'

'Oh God, I did forget that. Went clean out of my mind. I'll have to – '

'But, Ray, where are you? And what're you up to? Come on now, come clean.'

'London – but listen, not a word to anybody, Shell. Promise. Swear on – on your mother's head. Go on!'

'London! So you're on the trail of your mum, right? God, I just knew it, I just knew you'd found something out. But, you rotten friend, why didn't you tell me? Why didn't you take me with you? You know I'd've gone like a shot.'

'No you wouldn't! Or if you had come you'd've told everybody in advance and then the school would've found a way of stopping us – me, anyway. Shell, I just had to try this.'

'Well, come on then, tell me what's happened,' urged Shelley, ignoring the criticism. 'Have you found her? Is she coming home? I'm dying to know.'

'No, no luck yet but I've talked to somebody who's seen her recently. She must live round here, where I am at the moment, and so the trail's hotted up. She could even be just round the corner at this very minute. It's a bit weird, that feeling, but that is how I feel, Shell. I just *know* it's going to work out.'

'Well, great! But I'm just mad as hell I'm not with you to share it all out. I'm desperate to see your mum as well, you know. I want to know what she's been up to. Everyone at school will, too.'

That triggered a response to something Shelley had said earlier. 'Hey, listen, what did you mean when you said I'd caused a sensation at school? I mean, nobody could have a clue what I was up to, where I'd gone. So, what's going on?'

'Oh, it's just Mandy. Typical. She reckoned when she heard you were missing today that you would disappear too, just like your mum. You know, that you'd never come back. I suppose I shouldn't tell you this but it'll kill you. She said your dad had murdered *you* now he'd got away with murdering your mum! Course she was joking, Ray. Ray?'

Somehow Rachel managed to produce the semblance of a laugh. 'Oh yeah, *very* funny. Remind me to flatten Mandy when I catch up with her.' She paused, noting that her supply of money was rapidly running out. 'Listen, I'll have to go in a minute. No more money. Shell, I won't be back tomorrow, I've got to be here. But I'm absolutely certain I'll be back on

Thursday. So please just try and cover up for me till then. Say my dad's away but I've been really sick – food poisoning, anything that sounds convincing, OK?'

'I'll do my best, Ray. But take care, all right? I mean London's a desperate place. I don't want anything happening to my best mate. You are safe, aren't you?'

'Of course I am. I can take care of myself, you know that. Oh, I have met a flasher, though! Just – '

'What! Like the one we saw on top of the cliffs?'

Rachel's laugh was genuine this time. 'Well, not as obvious as him. This guy was on his own doorstep in his pyjamas so I was able to make a fast exit. That's been the only bad moment. But tomorrow's going to be the great day. Sorry, money's gone. See you, Shell.'

'Ray, ring – ' But the line was dead and whatever instruction she intended was lost.

Rachel walked slowly away from the kiosk. It was wonderful to be talking to Shelley but now she was completely alone again. Her enthusiasm for knocking on doors had waned. Soon people would be coming home to the square from work and Mum might be among them. So it might be a good idea to sit in the gardens with a view of the passers-by.

She sat and watched and saw nothing of the slightest interest to her. At one point an old man flourishing a cider bottle wandered along the path in front of her but she ignored him until he came too close. Then: 'Go away!' she hissed. To her surprise and relief, he did. A couple of dog walkers came by and then a schoolgirl in ankle socks. No one bothered her and gradually her pangs of hunger intensified.

Decisively, she stood up and returned to the ristorante. The proprietor was no longer on duty and she was served with her scrambled eggs on toast and a mug of cappuccino and an irresistible Russian slice by a sullen girl who did her best not to catch Rachel's eye even for a second. When she lingered over the coffee no one asked her if she wanted anything else. She could occupy her own world.

Would El really be there at 8 o'clock? She couldn't get the girl out of her mind and she knew she wanted to see her again. El had said Rachel would need her; that must have been a sort of come-on but now Rachel believed she did need her. For once, she didn't want to be on her own. Now that she'd failed in her search for Mum she needed to be with someone. Tonight, a stranger might be better than a friend.

She checked the time again and calculated how long she'd got before she arrived at the top of the steps leading from the Underground. 'Come on, action!' she told herself. There was one side of the square still un-investigated and now she was changing her tactics. All she'd do was check the names by the bell-pushes to see if there was a Blythe or anything like it. If nothing caught her interest then she'd abandon the square until the following morning. Her instincts told her that if luck was awaiting her then Mr Dalal would be the source; and her instincts also said that El would turn up.

The remaining homes yielded nothing apart from a chatty older woman who happened to open her door just as Rachel peered at the name-cards. Plainly she was glad of someone to talk to and she strove to bring

Janet to mind after seeing the photograph. But her honesty wouldn't allow her to invent something simply to keep her unexpected visitor on the doorstep (Rachel having declined an invitation to go in for a cup of something).

'Do call back in the morning because I'm sure I'll have remembered something useful by then,' the woman pleaded as Rachel at last managed to get away.

She was proud of her timing for it was two minutes to eight when she reached the entrance to the Underground station: and one minute later she saw El coming up the steps towards her.

9

To Rachel's surprise El was wearing an entirely different outfit from the one she'd had on earlier in the day: short, tight black skirt, bare legs and the black leather jacket Rachel had admired was now replaced by a dark-brown waist-length coat over a canary yellow sweater. The second surprise was that without a word being spoken El put her arms round Rachel and kissed her. It wasn't the kind of greeting she'd ever experienced from any of the girls she knew in Rocksea.

'Well, hi, I hoped I'd see you again,' Rachel, still a little shaken, told her. 'Have you been home to change since this morning, then?'

'I don't have a home, nowhere permanent, anyway,' said El, putting her arm through Rachel's and steering her into the opposite direction from Barossa Square. 'That's the way I want it. I just pick up what I fancy when I need it.'

'Oh,' replied Rachel, unable to think of anything more sensible to say in response to statements she didn't understand and didn't feel able at this stage to question. She knew already that El was going to remain an enigma until she wanted to explain herself.

'You want to come with me, don't you?' El inquired, turning her dark, brooding gaze on Rachel as, for a moment, they paused on their walk.

'Well, er, that depends. I mean, I've got to stay in London tonight. I've got money for an hotel and – '

'Don't waste it!' El cut in. 'You can kip with me. Just as good – better, 'cos you'll have me with you.'

Rachel had made up her mind that she didn't want to be alone; in spite of El's strangeness she was roughly Rachel's own age and therefore someone she thought she'd be safe with; her experience of hotels was practically non-existent and she'd certainly never stayed in one on her own.

'But where are we going?' she asked, trying to keep a hint of concern from her voice.

'You'll find out. You'll like it and we'll be together. You might meet a couple of mates of mine, Daisy and Vee.'

'Is, er, Vee a girl?' Rachel wondered.

'Course she is,' was the prompt reply, which immediately laid to rest one of Rachel's emerging fears. 'Girls should always stick together. That way we get what *we* want, right? You wouldn't let yourself be mucked about by guys, would you?'

'Definitely not!' Rachel replied resolutely, mainly because she felt it was what El wanted to hear.

At that moment a couple of youths, coming towards them, studied them from head to heels, their gazes clearly concentrating on their legs, Rachel's long and slim but El's thin as sticks (so thin that Rachel was half surprised she wore a skirt rather than the morning's trousers). El had seen what was

143

happening but wouldn't allow them to know it.

'That's guys,' she said conversationally as soon as they were out of earshot (but while they were still turning to see the rear view). 'Interested in only one thing. They won't get it from us, right?'

'Right,' agreed Rachel, thinking it a wonderfully protective remark. 'So, where're we heading, then, El?'

'You'll see in a minute, soon be there.'

Rachel would have been glad to shift her bag to the other shoulder but that would have meant dislodging El's companionable hold on her arm. Because she hadn't known whether she'd be staying overnight she'd brought some essential items with her and they fitted compactly into the bag. But after toting it around all day it was beginning to feel a burden. She hoped El's forecast of an arrival time was accurate.

They'd moved, almost imperceptibly, into an area of meaner streets, some featuring high concrete boxes completely out of character with the lines of plane trees in neighbouring avenues. The grander houses of Barossa Square seemed half a world away from these broken terraces and ranks of launderettes and take-aways and ethnic eating places and charity shops. Hardly anybody now seemed to show much interest in them as they moved along; and it occurred to Rachel they must seem such a pair that they were inseparable. It was odd really, because she never felt that way with Shelley when they were out 'testing the temperature', as Shell liked to describe it.

'Down here – let's get going,' El announced suddenly, releasing Rachel's arm and darting down a passageway flanked by high, dark grey brick walls.

She moved almost as if they were escaping pursuers, though she'd never once looked back on their way from the tube station.

Rachel hurried after her until El, with another rapid change of direction, shot through an arched gateway into what appeared to be somebody's back garden. Part of it was paved but there were also fruit bushes and a pair of apple trees. El, without slackening her pace, was now descending some steps leading from a flagged side path. When Rachel came up behind her El was carefully removing a long blonde hair, plainly not one of her own, from where it had been positioned across the door lock.

'Great, so nobody's been to bother us,' she announced, pushing the door inwards and disappearing.

Rachel suddenly felt wary. What was she going into? Who else was there? But she couldn't just stay outside and so she entered the gloomy basement. Before her eyesight could adjust to the darkness El was switching on a faint wall light.

'It's a squat!' Rachel exclaimed, taking in the bare floor, a pair of sleeping bags and a pile of scatter cushions. She'd never seen one in reality but it was almost identical to a place she'd seen on a TV documentary about the homeless.

'No, it's not, it's mine, all mine and this is how I like it,' El said lightly. 'Who needs dust-filled carpets and saggy old beds and stuff like that? It's what's in your head and your body that *really* matters.'

'Yes,' Rachel agreed less than enthusiastically. 'Is there, er, a bathroom?'

'Of course!' was the positive reply, made as if no

such question was necessary. 'Through that archway and at the bottom of the passage. Help yourself.'

'Thanks,' said Rachel in genuine relief, glad to have a few minutes to herself. Her day was becoming stranger by the minute. To her surprise, the bathroom was tidy and clean and spoilt only by a tidemark in the bath itself. There were towels and toothbrushes and even dental floss. So perhaps it wasn't a squat after all; perhaps it really was El's home, as she claimed. But how had she come by it and why was she so furtive when they arrived as if *she* was an intruder? Rachel would have liked to check out the other two rooms that opened off the passageway but didn't want to risk being caught in the act. El, she suspected, might easily react strongly if something displeased her.

El had thrown off her coat and was reclining on cushions, smoking a cigarette. She held out the packet, 'Want one?'

Rachel shook her head. 'I don't, thanks.'

'They're straight, you know, no dope,' El pointed out, faintly aggressive.

'No, no. I've never smoked anything, I just don't fancy it, that's all,' Rachel said defensively. She was beginning to feel she must appear to El to be a real country hick; yet she wanted to be completely different: sophisticated, poised, knowledgeable.

El shrugged and, a few moments later, got up and went to rummage in a cupboard that, Rachel now saw, was the base of a long, and quite elegant, windowseat. The only problem was that the window looked out on to a blank wall beside the steps to the basement.

'Want a drink, then?' El inquired, pouring some reddish liquid into a pair of tumblers.

Rachel swallowed her reservations. 'Yeah, thanks. Er, what is it?'

'Red wine, mostly. Got a kick, though. You'll like it. We drink it all the time, when we can afford it.'

Rachel swallowed and then coughed with the fire in the taste. Yet, moments later, the mellowness of the wine provided a glow of enjoyment. The second sip wasn't nearly as fierce.

'It's good,' she nodded as El returned to the cupboard and this time came back with a very large see-through bag of doughnuts. She wasn't the slightest bit hungry but it seemed companionable to take a doughnut; it would also help to soak up the wine, she reasoned, and that might not be a bad thing.

El, devouring a doughnut at speed, snuggled up to her on the cushions. 'So, what you doing in London, then?' she asked, her dark gaze boring into Rachel's eyes.

Rachel wanted to say, 'I thought you'd never ask,' but didn't; instead, she began to tell the story of her quest for her mother and how it had all started with Janet's abrupt disappearance from home. It felt strange to be relating all this to someone she'd never seen until a few hours ago and who knew nothing whatsoever about her or her family. El listened without interrupting once, except to nod now and again or, occasionally, open her eyes wide in apparent surprise. Her expression didn't alter and her gaze was constant. Rachel had never known anyone pay her so much concentrated attention; and that alone would have kept her talking.

When she hadn't a cigarette in her hand El from time to time allowed her hand to stray to Rachel's hair, combing it or smoothing it with long fingers. It was a very long time since anyone had touched her so intimately, perhaps since the last time her mother embraced her after bad news about a school exam. She was surprised, at one stage, to find El refilling her glass; she hadn't realized she'd emptied it. By now they'd munched their way through half the doughnuts, too.

'So, what do *you* think, El?' Rachel stopped suddenly to ask. 'I mean, you haven't expressed a single opinion, have you? I'm glad – it's terrific – that you'll just listen to me meandering on and on. But, well, I do want to know what you *think*.'

El shrugged but still kept her free arm round Rachel's shoulders. 'Don't know, do I, why she bunked off like that? If you don't, how can I have a clue? Don't think it's important, really. Parents are a waste of time. Haven't seen mine for years and I'm no worse off. You won't be, either, girl.'

Rachel didn't have the energy or inclination to argue. But it felt funny, really funny, to be called 'girl' in that way. 'Listen, you've never asked me my name, have you? And I don't know yours – only El.'

'Names don't matter. Best to call yourself what you like. I do. Doesn't make any difference to how I feel about you if I know your name.'

'Suppose not,' Rachel mumbled. She knew she was mumbling but she didn't seem to have the strength to speak properly again. Suddenly, she was tired, bone-achingly tired. She took a deep pull at her drink: and this time it had a different taste. Sharp again but then meltingly easy to swallow all the way down.

'You – did you – did you – give me a – a different – taste – taste – I mean – drink?' she could hear herself saying even though it was such an effort to speak at all.

'Good, ain't it?' she thought she heard El say, now speaking from far, far away.

She was helpless to save herself from falling into the deepest sleep of her life. She knew she was about to slide sideways and she put her arms out so that she could hold on to El; and she thought El took care of her. But she didn't really know what was happening for by then she was unconscious.

It was hard, almost impossible, to swallow. Her throat seemed to have closed up completely. Somehow, she managed it and the discomfort made her retch. Her eyes flickered open once but closed again immediately. The light was painful, though all she could see was a blur.

Rachel knew her mind wasn't functioning properly, either. Her tongue tentatively explored her lips, seeking moisture; but her lips were as dry as her throat. She hadn't felt as bad as this since – since – but she couldn't remember that, either.

'Think!' she ordered. 'Think!' But a drink was the greater priority; she must find something to ease the state of her throat. This time she managed to keep her eyes open a fraction longer. The light was dim but she could make out the shape of what could be a window over to her right. That was the source of the light.

She tried to climb out of bed but found she was

already on the floor, and so she managed only to roll over, pushing aside the thin blanket covering her. She got to her knees and then somehow, for there was nothing to grasp to help her up, to her feet. It was then she discovered she wasn't wearing anything.

Suddenly, memory returned. She knew where she was and what had been happening before she fell asleep. 'El!' she called; or tried to call, for only a croak emerged from her seized-up throat. 'El!' she said again, a little louder this time. 'Where are you?'

But already she sensed she was alone, that there'd be no reply. Because she didn't know where her clothes were and she needed a drink more than anything else in the world she stumbled across the room, tripping once so badly over a cushion she fell to her knees on the wooden boards of the floor.

Thankfully, the bathroom was where she thought it was and she drank straight from the tap before splashing water against her eyes and over her face. Chilled now, she made her way back to the main room and discovered her clothes, neatly folded, on the shelf at the head of the makeshift bed. As she put them on she tried to work out why El – for it must have been she; anything else was unthinkable – had removed them. Was it because she didn't want them to crease badly while Rachel slept; or was there a sinister motive? Rachel shivered at that thought and tried to concentrate on what El might be doing now. Had she, perhaps, gone out for food for them? Rachel had seen it was just after 8 o'clock (which meant she must have slept for about ten hours, although she couldn't be sure how much time had passed while she was drinking with El the previous evening).

'My money!' Suddenly she remembered the emergency fund of notes she had so carefully folded inside her bra, a place of total safety, she'd believed. And now she'd put her bra on again she knew it was missing. Was that why El had undressed her, in order to search for anything of value Rachel might be carrying? She remembered slipping her shoulder bag off and putting it on the window seat. Her heart leapt in relief when she saw it was still there. But it took only seconds to learn that all her money had gone – well, except for a solitary pound coin, loose in the bottom of the bag. Had El left her that in a moment of compassion or just overlooked it?

Rachel sank down into the cushions again, her legs feeling as if they hadn't the strength to support her. How could she have been so stupid as to trust a total stranger like El? Why hadn't she sensed that the girl was just on the make? No answers came and yet question after question piled up in her mind. Was there anyone in the world who could be trusted? Mum had let her down – and her father – and that horrible man who'd answered the door in Barossa Square – and now the girl she really believed wanted to befriend her. She was left completely on her own without enough money to buy herself a meal. A small chocolate bar and maybe a cup of tea, that's all £1 would run to in London. She was finished. Rachel's chin sank on to her knees as she hugged her bare legs. What was she going to do now? Without money she could do nothing. If only she'd brought her building society paybook with her – except that almost certainly El would have stolen that, too. She might just as well admit defeat and go home and confess to total defeat. So, she should get herself to King's Cross and catch the next train.

Her ticket! 'Oh God, not that, too!' she exclaimed aloud. Back to her bag, scrabble through contents and – 'Well, at least I've got that!'

Plainly a return rail ticket to Rocksea had been of no value to El. But then, Rachel thought wryly, who would want to take a day trip to Rocksea out of season? After all, she didn't want to return there and it was her home. Or, more accurately, she didn't want to go back with a tale of total failure in London. Shelley, for one, would demand every possible detail Rachel could dredge up of what had transpired, who she'd talked to, what she'd seen, who she'd fancied, who'd fancied her. She'd have to be very careful what she disclosed about El. So she needed *some* success to report, *something* to look back on with a sense of triumph, however minor it was in truth.

Rachel returned to the bathroom to have a quick shower. The water, surprisingly, was lukewarm, which meant someone must be paying the fuel bills. Her throat was almost normal after a long drink of tap water and she was beginning to come alive again. Her thoughts insisted on flicking back to El: had she really befriended her only to rob her? If so, she must have planned it meticulously in spite of giving the impression that she always acted on impulse and just lived for the day. Did El really live in this strange basement (plainly somebody did) or had she just 'borrowed' it for the night? Would she return? Not for days, until the coast was clear, Rachel reasoned. And where was El now: haunting tube platforms for other easy victims? Or might she be hanging about Barossa Park Station, a place that obviously had some appeal to her? Of course, she might have selected it as a rendezvous because Rachel had said it was where she was going.

'Stop thinking about her!' Rachel admonished herself as she finished dressing. 'Forget her.' But she couldn't, even after leaving the basement and making her way back to Barossa Square. Although she'd been concentrating on El and their conversation on their walk in the reverse direction she'd taken some note of the route for she found no difficulty in retracing her steps. By now she was beginning to feel hungry; it was, after all, a long time since she'd had a real meal. But hunger, too, had to be suppressed: she had no means of allaying it unless, perhaps, she met the dress designer again and could borrow money from her. She was the only person Rachel could think of who might help her.

The square was as quiet as it had been for much of the previous day. Plenty of people were using the crossings on the corners on their way to work or wherever else they were going; but not many people were in the square itself. By now Rachel could imagine what went on behind the secured doors of the elegant Georgian houses. There were still many she hadn't tackled but that seemed a hopeless task. In any case, she had one lead to pursue.

Deliberately she crossed her fingers as she approached All Hours, praying that Mr Dalal was back at work. If she couldn't speak to him then her last hope was extinguished. There'd be no point in staying in London any longer for the odds against catching sight of Mum around the square were too stupefyingly high to consider.

To Rachel's great surprise the shop was so busy there was a queue at the check-out. The lank-haired girl was still the one taking the money and there was no sign of a man who might be Mr Dalal. 'But he might be having his tea break, might be making a cup of tea for the girl, anything,' she encouraged herself, although without conviction. She wondered whether she dare break into the queue just to ask the girl about her chances of seeing the proprietor today. She glanced round again, hoping he might in that moment be coming through the door behind her, smiling and happy to answer all her questions and tell her precisely where she could find her mother.

And it was then that her eye caught the swinging see-through plastic sleeve of personal advertisements on the door itself, swinging because a departing customer had brushed against it. And she saw the familiar signature: Janet.

Suddenly, her mouth was dry again: and she felt faint, not now from lack of food. Her hand was trembling as she stilled the sleeve and read the typed words on the white card:

Caring baby-sitter available day-time or evening. Any age of child considered. References available from 14 Bonthorn Place. Janet.

*

And, as if to endorse the message, the card was signed with a black felt-tip pen with Mum's traditional flourish. Her mother, working as a *baby-sitter*? Caring for someone else's child, or children, maybe, after she'd abandoned her own daughter? That was what struck Rachel immediately. How could she do such a thing? And why had she *wanted* to do it?

'Excuse me,' a voice roughly came at her. 'Are you in the queue or what? I mean, you're making a good job of blocking the entrance.'

'Oh, sorry.' Rachel didn't feel sorry at all because the man talking to her was making a fuss for nothing. He could easily get by and it was plain she wasn't part of the queue. Some men were always antagonistic to young persons. Still, he might have his uses.

'Do you know where Bonthorn Place is, please?'

He glared but rapped out an answer. 'Opposite side of the square – diagonally opposite – down Farrer's Row – second, no third, on the right – Bonthorn Mews down to the bottom, turn right. That's it.'

She was astonished by such precision as well as knowledge. 'Thanks – thanks a lot,' she told him, rewarding him with her most dazzling smile. It was the first smile of any kind she'd managed for hours. She hurtled out of All Hours, not stopping her headlong run until she reached the far side of Barossa Square. Just the sight of her mother's name, the familiar signature, had revitalized her. Surely her quest was over now? Surely this couldn't be another false trail? But now that her emotions were under control her intelligence took over. She knew she could shortly be facing the final disappointment, the final blow: no answer from anyone at 14 Bonthorn Place or someone who had never even heard of Janet Blythe.

In Farrer's Row she slowed almost to a halt: she knew now she should have asked the girl in the check-out about the advertisement. Did she know who'd put it in? Could she describe her? Was it so old that by now Janet might have moved out of the area?

'Please, please let her be there!' she prayed fervently under her breath.

In Bonthorn Mews she paused more than once yet was hardly aware of the glistening black paint on huge garage doors that seemed to occupy the entire frontage of the two-storey cottages. Because she wasn't really looking where she was going she stumbled on the cobbled surface where it dipped into a drainage channel to simulate the kind of roadway that existed when the mews really was home for horses and carriages.

She was steeling herself against rejection, believing it was the likeliest of all the possibilities she might encounter at 14 Bonthorn Place. As Mum had turned against her once, simply by disappearing without warning or explanation, why shouldn't she reject her again if she answered the door? She couldn't really imagine Mum seeing her and then slamming the door shut in her face; but then, she must have been acting out of character lately anyway. So Rachel had to be prepared for almost anything to happen.

The houses in Bonthorn Place were altogether different from those in the mews, a mixture of modern and Edwardian but, as ever in London, jumbled so close together it was sometimes hard to tell one from another. Number 14 was approached by a flight of steps from a paved area in front of a walkway bordered by plane trees and the predominant colour was battleship grey relieved by shining white. Rachel took all this in because she had to stand and study the house before summoning up courage to climb the steps and ring the bell. She still couldn't convince herself that her search was over. Perhaps the signature on the advert wasn't Mum's at all. In her haste, her anxiety, to find some trace of her she'd accepted a near likeness as the real thing. Then she shook her head to clear such doubts and ascended.

And rang the bell.

10

In the few moments before there was an answer Rachel thought about turning away and racing down the steps so that she wouldn't see who opened the door. There'd been so many huge disappointments in her life she didn't think she could face another. It was better not to know the worst. But she couldn't move: she remained rooted to the spot, listening to the sounds of a chain being unhooked and a key turned in the lock. Her heart was thumping madly again.

A girl a few years older than herself opened the door and greeted Rachel with a sort of polite smile reserved for unexpected callers. Then her expression changed to one of apparent recognition. Her first words confirmed it.

'Oh, hello,' she said, almost conversationally. 'You must be Rachel. Yes?'

Rachel was flabbergasted. 'How – how d'you know my name? And who are you?'

There was a momentary pause before the girl answered: 'Oh, I know your name from M– from Janet. Oh, and I'm Helen.'

Rachel was beginning to feel faint, without quite knowing why for it wasn't just lack of breakfast. She

sensed, rather than knew, there was something familiar about this girl. And Helen, she saw, was looking at
her with a fierce intentness as if she'd never seen a
human face before and was determined to commit it to
memory for the rest of her life. So it took a second or
two before Rachel realized she had found someone
who really was in contact with her mother.

'Does my mum work here, then?' she inquired
tentatively. 'Work for you, I mean, or your family?'

'Well, not exactly,' said Helen, her smile widening
across her heart-shaped face. 'Look, you'd better come
in. I think we've got a lot to talk about. OK?'

She moved aside before the invitation could be
declined and Rachel, nodding her thanks, stepped into
the entrance hall and hesitated until Helen added: 'Just
go straight ahead. The sitting-room's facing you. Be
with you in a second.'

The room was ordinary enough and there were no
photographs on display that might have yielded clues
to the people who lived in this house. Rachel perched
on the edge of a three-seat sofa and tried to imagine
why Helen had left her alone. Was she intending to
return with Janet? Was Mum actually in the house at
this moment? Rachel's hopes began to rise again.
Surely her search was about to end?

The moment Helen returned Rachel knew she'd
been brushing her shoulder-length light brown hair
and, probably, checking her eye-shadow and make-up
(it was, after all, what she would've done herself if
their roles had been reversed). But now her manner
was less confident: she was, Rachel guessed, nervous.
So what else had she been up to in the past few

moments? Talking to someone about their unexpected visitor? Telephoning Janet, or trying to?

'Look, as you know my name you must know who I am, that I'm Janet's daughter, I mean,' Rachel said eagerly as Helen sank into a matching armchair opposite her. 'I've come all the way to London to find Mum, find out why she just left us at home and disappeared. I'm desperate to know what's happened so please help me. Don't drag out the suspense for me any longer if you know about her, what she's doing, where I can see her. Please, Helen. And tell me how you know her, who you are.'

The girl flicked hair back from her shoulders and then ran her long fingers down the seams of her black trousers, a mannerism that Rachel recognized as either a delaying tactic or an indication of nerves. Then Helen looked at her with a directness that showed she'd made up her mind what to say.

'Look, Rachel, there's no other way of telling you this. I know it's going to be a shock but' – there was a fractional pause but her voice remained firm as she added – 'I am your sister. Well, half-sister, naturally. But your sister all the same.'

Rachel, who'd been preparing herself for news that might easily have been the worst she'd ever heard in her life, couldn't speak at all for a moment or two. Her mind was in a whirl but still functioning. 'You mean my mum is – *your* mum, too?'

Helen nodded, her dark brown eyes not losing their concentration on Rachel's face. 'Yes. Look, I know you must be almost knocked-out to discover my existence in this way but, well, I'm thrilled to meet you at last. I truly am, Rachel. I've wanted to see you for years and years. And now – '

'You mean, *you* have known about me while I never knew a thing about you?' Rachel exclaimed, indignation now mingling with astonishment. She wanted to know everything, everything she possibly could about all that had been going on through the years that must have impinged on her own relationship with Mum. It still hadn't sunk in that she possessed the sister she'd always wanted, but she could explore her feelings about that later.

'Well, yes, but, you see, I didn't really know that you didn't know about me,' Helen said, nibbling the inside of her lower lip. 'I sort of assumed that Janet – Mum – would confide in you because you were with her all the time. My other mum, the one I used to think was my real mum, Pam, well, she used to tell me all sorts of secrets all the time when I was little and when I was growing up. So – '

'But who's your dad?' Rachel burst in. 'I mean, was my mum married before she met my dad? I can't believe that. Somebody would have said something. I'd've heard something from somebody.'

For the first time since she'd come into the sitting-room Helen allowed her gaze to drift away from Rachel; she didn't answer at once and Rachel began to wonder what on earth she was going to hear next.

'My dad's dead, he died not so long after I was born, so I never knew him,' Helen said in a flat voice. 'Your dad's at home, isn't he, he's alive and well?'

'Er, yes, that's right,' agreed Rachel, experiencing a sense of guilt at having had the luxury of both parents at home while Helen had had neither. Yet who was Pam? And, even more intriguing, who was Helen's father? 'But who was your dad?' she asked again.

Once more, Helen glanced away, across to the window that overlooked Bonthorn Place as if seeking help with her answers. 'Well, he was Janet's boyfriend when they were at school and his name was Simon. They started me – by *accident*, of course – when they were both in the sixth form. Mum – Janet – had to drop out of school when it – I – became obvious. Her parents were horrified at what she'd done. They probably wanted her to get rid of it, though Janet won't say much about that, even now.'

She was speaking quite slowly and Rachel wished she'd hurry up because she wanted to know everything as fast as possible; there were questions she couldn't wait to ask but she daren't risk interrupting Helen's amazing story.

'Well, Janet wasn't going to get rid of her baby – and Simon didn't want her to, either,' Helen went on, though she was now directly looking at Rachel. 'He was going to university, wanted to become a scientist and make great discoveries to help the world. I've been told he was quite keen to marry Janet but seemingly everyone advised him he was too young and ought to wait until at least he was through his university course. So – '

'But what about Mum?' Rachel couldn't prevent herself cutting in. 'I mean, did she want to marry him? And, well, *did* they marry?'

Now Helen looked taken aback. 'Well, of course they didn't. That's really why there's been all this secrecy all these years. I thought you'd know that – I mean that your mum hadn't been married before she married Roy. For one thing, there really wasn't time.'

'Oh,' was all Rachel could manage. It was hard to come to terms with the fact that Helen had so much more knowledge of Janet's present life as well as of her past. Yet she, Rachel, who had lived with her mum for all the years of her life, knew scarcely anything of Janet's earlier history. 'So, well, what happened to Mum – and your dad – when you were born?'

'As I said, Janet's parents didn't want to know her after she started me and so they more or less threw her out. That's when she went to live with Pam, Simon's mum. So Pam is really my grandmother, though all my life she's acted as my mum. For years and years I never knew she wasn't my true mother. Actually, I still think of her like that in spite of recognizing Janet as my biological mum. So even when I got to know about you I didn't envy you, Rachel. The only thing I wished was that I had a dad, too. But as I've never had one I suppose I haven't missed him, not like so many kids these days who are in one-parent families because their dad went off with somebody else. It must be like that at your school, right?'

Rachel nodded. 'It definitely is. But, Helen, what happened to your dad, Simon? I mean, he didn't go off with anybody else, did he?'

'Sometimes I wish he had,' Helen said with a wry smile, 'because then he might still be alive. No, he was killed in a car crash, a car driven by a mate of his. They were celebrating someone's birthday at university. That's where they were, in Manchester. Never had a chance – killed outright. And I was only six months old. Mum – I mean Pam – well, she's never really got over it. He was her only son, only child. She didn't have a husband much longer, either. My grandad – he was called Jim – he was a lot older than Pam and he'd been ill for years, I'm told. He died a couple of years after Simon was killed. But at least he left her fairly well off. So we haven't done badly for money and the house is Mum's.'

'But what happened to my mum, Janet, after Simon was killed?' Rachel wanted to know. She felt guilty at glossing over Helen's and Pam's tragedies but she needed to find out how her mother had coped with the disasters in her own life at an age when she was probably little older than Helen now.

'Well, she could simply have gone on living with Pam if she'd wanted to, I know that from what Mum – sorry, Pam – has told me. But instead she felt the whole world was against her, everything had gone wrong for her. She says she couldn't cope any more. So she left, just took off for the north. But without me, of course.'

Rachel stared at her sister, shaken yet again by what she was hearing. So her mum's recent disappearance from Rocksea wasn't the first time she'd run away! She'd even deserted her baby, a helpless, fatherless infant!

Helen was holding up a warning hand. 'Hang on, Rachel! I can tell what you're thinking but it wasn't as bad as that. I mean, Pam was perfectly happy to look after me, to bring me up as her own child, if you like. After all, she'd lost Simon – and I was Simon's love-child. So she wanted to love me in his place. She's said that many, many times. She didn't have other children, as I told you, and her husband, well, he was sick most of the time. There wasn't a lot she could do for him except make him as comfortable as possible. But I represented a new life, literally. That's how she puts it. So she could cope whereas Janet really couldn't, mainly because she was so young. So, that's the way it was.'

'But what did Mum do, where did she go?'

Instead of answering Helen glanced at her wristwatch and then stood up. 'Look, do you want a drink? I know I could do with one. I'm beginning to feel drymouthed!'

'Oh yes, thanks, that'd be great,' Rachel replied, recognizing that a drink was exactly what she needed. She was also feeling distinctly hungry.

'Good, I'll go and put the kettle on – won't be a moment.'

'Oh, I'll come with you, if you don't mind,' Rachel volunteered eagerly. 'Then we can go on talking. I must have a thousand questions to ask and after that I'll probably think of some more!'

Helen laughed. 'Well, I don't know that I'll have the answers. But you're free to ask. Come on, the kitchen's this way.'

As she followed down the corridor Rachel couldn't help being aware that she was a couple of inches taller than her sister and somehow that pleased her. Very likely it would take her a long time to get used to having an older sister, someone who'd had a totally different life from her own and looked so different and even talked in a different accent. And yet – they had so much in common; in genetic terms they were almost as close as any two people could be. Rachel, as she looked admiringly round the small but beautifully fitted kitchen, was surprised to discover how excited she was feeling about the future in spite of all the worries swirling through her mind.

'It's lovely,' she said politely. 'I think even *I* could really enjoy doing the cooking in here. Do you like cooking, or does you mum – sorry! Pam – do it all?' Rachel cursed herself for that slip but it was going to take time to adjust to these surprising relationships. Fortunately, Helen didn't seem to mind.

'Actually, I *do* like creating some things, sauces and special puddings, oh, and the occasional curry with all the accompaniments. When I've got time, that is. Do you want tea or coffee? And anything to eat? When did you have breakfast? You must have left Rocksea pretty early to get here by now. Or did you stay in London overnight?' She paused and laughed again. 'Listen to me! I've got into the questioning groove now!'

'Coffee, thanks, and yes, I'm starving, to be honest. I didn't manage to get any breakfast, so – '

'Well, come on, then, have something good! What'd you like? Cheese on toast, omelette, scrambled eggs – '

'How about a cheese omelette? That'd be best. Plenty of protein, and they keep going on about protein at school.'

School was the subject of the next set of questions from Helen as she deftly grated cheese and cracked eggs and got on with the mixing process. Rachel, answering most of them either flippantly or earnestly, was able to study her sister as she worked. What they

166

definitely had in common, she could see, was high cheekbones and probably much the same colouring, although Helen clearly used more make-up. She's my *sister*, Rachel kept reminding herself in between questions and answers, she really is my sister – but I can hardly believe it. Suddenly it occurred to her that it was going to be wonderfully exciting telling Shelley all the things that had happened to her in London, the bad as well as the good, but above all, about Helen.

'Right, tuck in, Rachel,' her sister invited, sliding the plate in front of her on the breakfast bar before pouring mugs of coffee. 'And when your mouth isn't full tell me this: did Mum, our mum, never give you a hint of my existence? Did you never suspect anything, well, unusual about her past?'

'Definitely not,' Rachel declared, hastily swallowing another mouthful so that Helen shouldn't think she was covering anything up by delaying her answer. 'I've tried to get her to talk about her life when she was a teenager but she insisted there was nothing to tell, her school life and family were just too boring to remember.'

Helen nodded. 'Yeah, I can imagine she would. She's still pretty cautious with us, too, even though we've explored a lot of territory since she came down to see me – well, us. Pam was the opposite, really, she told me when I was quite young that she wasn't my real mum. She explained everything and I just accepted it. I mean, I'd lost my dad so why not my mum? It didn't matter. Not for a long time. But then, well, I did begin to want to know about Janet, wanted to see her. Pam said it was best not to because Janet didn't want it. They were in touch by phone some-times, so I gather. But there were times when I just wished my real mother would come home to see me, to show me she cared something for me. Pam knew how I felt, she's clever like that, and she said it would happen one day, no doubt about it. And it has, and now you've come, too. I'm glad about that, Rachel, really glad. I've seen a picture of you – Janet keeps one in her purse, doesn't she? – but you're much prettier than your picture. And taller, quite a bit taller.'

For the first time since they'd met less than half an hour ago Rachel felt embarrassed. She wanted to pay her own compliments but sensed that now they would sound either false or too fulsome, as if she were sim-ply being polite. So she smiled as warmly as she could, swallowed more omelette and came up with the ques-tion she'd intended to ask the moment she was invited into the house. 'Listen, why did Mum come to see you *now*? And why couldn't she tell us what was happen-ing? I mean, I'd've been thrilled to know about you. I wouldn't have felt jealous or anything stupid like that. I suppose, though, that Dad might have been a prob-lem. If – '

'Do you think he knows about me? About Mum's – Janet's – relationship with Simon?'

Rachel shook her head. 'Doubt it. No, I'm sure he doesn't. He's pretty secretive, too, I really think I have secret service agents for parents! But I can't believe it wouldn't have emerged in some conversation or row or argument or whatever.'

'Don't they, your parents, get on?' Helen inquired gently. 'Sorry, Rachel, I'm not prying into things that don't concern me. It's just that, as I say, I don't know the sort of things most girls would normally know about their own families.'

'Me too!' Rachel said fervently; and then laughed to dispel any tension. 'To be honest, I haven't a clue about how they really get on, except that they don't seem to hate each other or anything drastic like that. So far as I can tell they just trundle along together in the same way they've probably always done.'

There didn't seem to be anything more she could usefully say and, smiling again, she pushed her plate away. 'That was really great, Helen, thanks. Enjoyed every mouthful. You could get a job as a cook in a posh restaurant anywhere. Listen, do you have a job?'

'Not at the moment,' Helen replied, suddenly looking away again. 'I did have, though: I was a nurse – still am, really – in a private hospital. But, well, I decided I needed a break. I've got other plans for the future.'

Rachel, remembering she still hadn't been given an answer to an earlier question, had a flash of insight. 'Is that why Mum's come to see you now, because of what you're planning?'

'Well, yes, actually. I wanted to see her, anyway, I told you that. And this is the first time we've met since – since I was just a small baby.'

For the first time it seemed to Rachel that Helen was upset by what she was telling her. Rachel reached out and squeezed her sister's hand. She would have liked to put her arms round her but feared it might be too soon for that.

'But why didn't she tell me and Dad what she was

up to?' Rachel asked, half-speaking to herself. 'What's the point of keeping something as important as this a secret?'

Helen, in control of her emotions again, shrugged. 'I can't tell you that, Rachel. Only Janet can answer that. You can ask her yourself. She should be back here before long. Any time now, really.'

Rachel's eyes opened wide. 'She's staying here? Mum's staying *here*, with you?'

'No, no, not with us but fairly close in Barossa Square. She's – '

'Yes, I knew that,' Rachel cut in. 'That's how I traced her – and through the advert she has in that shop, All Hours. I came here because this is the address for references, or so the advert said. I don't understand that at all.'

Helen sighed. 'Oh well, there's nothing complicated about it, though I suppose it must sound a bit odd to you now. When Janet agreed to come down to see us we would've been happy for her to stay with us but she didn't want that. She insisted it would be fairer if she paid her way and also had a bit of space to herself, you know, to get used to seeing us, to get used to us, in fact. She wanted to earn some money and the only easy way of getting cash in your hand is to look after children. So that's what she decided to do and Mum – Pam – was willing to provide a reference if anyone demanded one. So far I don't think anyone has, they're all just so pleased to get hold of a reliable woman who can look after their kids during the day without any hassle. And Janet does seem good at that. Must be because she was good at bringing you up, Rachel.'

She said that in a matter-of-fact way, without any hint of irony or envy in her voice, and Rachel didn't make any comment. To her, though, it seemed strange that her mother should abandon her to go off and look after kids belonging to complete strangers.

'Anyway, it's worked well,' Helen resumed. 'Janet's had her independence and we've got to know her well. She and Mum – sorry, Pam! Look, I'd better just use their real names all the time and that'll solve the identity problem. As I was about to say, Pam and Janet actually get on really well: I know they like each other. Apparently they always did when Simon was Janet's boyfriend and Pam didn't turn against her when she became pregnant with me. I can think of plenty of mothers who'd've had a totally different attitude if their son announced his girlfriend was pregnant. They're out together now, shopping.'

Rachel didn't know what to say: everything she was hearing was a surprise, so she shouldn't have been surprised to learn that her mum and her sister's grandmother had gone shopping together. But she was. Somehow it characterized the bizarre nature of all the circumstances surrounding her own life at present.

'How do you and Mum – Janet – get on with each other? Now you've spent time together, I mean?' she asked, not wanting to make the question seem more important than it was.

'Oh, pretty well, I think,' Helen answered in a contemplative tone. 'I mean, I know I like her and I think she likes me. Rachel, why don't we take our coffee into the sitting-room? It's more comfortable there. Unless there's something else you'd like to eat?'

'No, no, that was great, thanks. Just what I needed.'
It occurred to Rachel that Helen might want a moment
or two to reflect on what else she should say about the
relationship with her real mother and so the move
from one room to another was a useful interval.

'Rachel, this is hard to say and I don't know whether
I'll be able to explain it properly,' Helen resumed
quietly as she again sat opposite her in one of the
floral-patterned blue and green armchairs. 'When I
knew Janet was coming to see us I worried, couldn't
help it, that we might not get on, might not even like
each other. I mean, there's no law, is there, that says
you have to like your own children? I'm sure she felt
much the same as I did in advance and that's why she
wanted her own place. Then, you see, if things didn't
work out, well, she could just return home and resume
her normal life. And you and your dad wouldn't be
any the wiser. I know this sounds, well – '

'No, no, I understand and I'm sure you're right.
That's how Mum is. It's always been hard to know
what she really feels or wants. That's why we hadn't a
clue where she'd gone when she disappeared. Or, of
course, *why*.'

Helen, twisting a ring on her finger and biting her
lip at the apparent complexity of people's lives, nodded her sympathy. 'You must have been out of your
minds. Did you go to the police to get them to trace
her?'

'Oh sure, though I was keener on that than Dad
was. You see, in a way he thought she was entitled to
do anything she liked and so, if she ran away, well,
that was her business. Actually, he doesn't know

where I am, either. I bunked off school just for a day – two at the most – because it seemed to me the only way I was going to find Mum was to do it myself. The police, you see, can't do anything: no crime's been committed and any person is free to go off and do their own thing if they want. So if Dad couldn't be bothered to search for Mum he certainly won't be out looking for me! We get on all right but nothing special. I've always been closer to Mum even if that hasn't been – '

She broke off as she heard a key turning in a lock and then a door opening. Helen, too, reacted immediately, swinging her legs from under her and rising from her chair.

'Darling, we're back!' a female voice called cheerfully. 'And guess what – Janet's managed to find her outfit!'

Helen, now on her feet, called out: 'I'm in here – and Rachel's with me.'

Rachel, too, was standing, ready to greet Pam as she came into the room. But, suddenly, it was her mother who was there, as startled as Rachel herself by what was happening, but opening her arms to receive her as Rachel flung herself forward. As they embraced the tears began to flow simultaneously for both of them.

'Oh, Ray, I'm so glad to see you again,' Janet murmured when, at last, she could detach herself. 'I was going to phone you today – yes, honestly! There's just no need to wait any longer, not now. But how did you find me? How on earth did you manage it?'

'Well, I got a clue about Barossa Square and I worked it out from there,' said Rachel, just about composed enough now to remember her vow to herself not to reveal to anyone that she'd tampered with Ted's mail. Her parents had their secrets so she would keep hers.

Janet, though, was not really listening. She'd become aware that Rachel had never met Pam and yet Pam was now obliged to be a mere spectator in her own home while Janet and Rachel celebrated their reunion.

'Pam, I'm sorry I haven't intro – ' Janet was starting to say when Pam, shrugging aside superfluous apologies, moved forward and put her arms round Rachel and kissed her.

'I'm so glad to meet you at last, Rachel, because I've thought about you often, especially lately,' said Pam warmly.

Rachel smiled, not really knowing what to say. Pam was different from what she'd begun to imagine since Helen had talked about her. She was plump and although her short, wavy brown hair was highlighted by touches of silvery-grey she looked a little too young to have been the mother of Janet's boyfriend, Simon. Perhaps, though, Rachel reflected, bringing up a grandchild almost on her own had helped keep her youthful.

'I'm sure you two'd like a drink – Rachel and I have just had one – so I'll get it,' Helen volunteered; and, diplomatically, Pam said she needed the bathroom. And so Rachel and her mother were left on their own.

They sank together on to the sofa, Janet taking one of Rachel's hands in her own and then hugging her tightly again. They both had tears to blink back or brush aside though Rachel was experiencing a calmness she hadn't known for months.

'Mum, why didn't you tell us? About Helen, I mean. Couldn't you tell I'd've loved to hear I had a sister? You even used to tell me sometimes that I was unlucky I was always on my own, that I just had parents and no one else. And all the time there was Helen, here in London. So why, *why*?'

Janet's sigh was a familiar sound to Rachel. 'Oh, I know, I wanted to. Desperately sometimes. But, well, much of the time I've just had to force her out of my mind, told myself to concentrate on you.' She paused as if uncertain what to say next. So Rachel, determined to learn as much as possible before Helen and Pam returned, pressed her: 'But did Dad never suspect anything? How could you keep it from him?'

'Oh, I've always realized it's not been fair on him. But, you know, husbands and wives don't always provide their partners with full details of previous encounters or romances. Too often that's a recipe for disaster or at least jealousy! Discreet silence can be best.'

'Yes, OK,' Rachel agreed exasperatedly, 'but in this case there was Helen. That's a bit different from just an old romance that didn't come to anything, isn't it?'

'True. Well, I couldn't hurt him by telling him after you were born, that would've been terrible for him. You were all that mattered to us both. I'd given Helen up. Has she told you all about herself and Pam and, and me?'

'Yes, most of it, I should think. Well, most of what she knows or has been told.'

'Good, that's a relief, a weight off my mind, really.

Well, as I was saying, we had you and the future to think about. People shouldn't live in the past and I'd vowed not to. I suspect your dad has always thought there was someone special in my life before he came along but he's been very considerate and said nothing. Well, nothing that meant he was probing into my past. Your dad's always been content with the present. He's not really interested in the past. And, anyway, you know he lives in a world of figures, not people. So the longer the silence about Helen lasted then the harder it was going to be to reveal the truth. Darling, you must understand that. I did what I did for the best, thinking of you above all. You can accept that, Ray, can't you?'

Rachel nodded. 'I expect so. I mean, there's a lot I've had to accept since you went away, and also since I got to London. But Dad, well, I can't quite imagine what he'll say, or do, when he hears all this.'

Her mother murmured: 'Nor can I, to tell the truth. How is he?'

'Same as usual, I suppose, unworried. Or that's how he always appears, isn't it?'

Janet laughed. 'I knew it! That's why I didn't worry about him when I left. I worried only about you. But you're a survivor. Like me, really. You'll adapt to a situation and make the most of it, whatever it is. I'm right, aren't I?'

'Well, I don't know about that,' Rachel replied, frowning. 'I didn't have any choice over this, did I? It's not easy at school, I can tell you. People were sympathetic at first but then as time went on lots would make funny remarks about whose fault it was when there was no sign of you coming back. That's why I had to come and find you, I couldn't go on not knowing anything, even feeling guilty because for all I knew it could have been my fault.'

Her mother's grip on her shoulder tightened in a sympathetic squeeze. 'Oh darling, I am sorry. But I just couldn't tell you because I'd no idea how things might turn out down here. There was so much I had to know first, from Pam as well as Helen. But now it's all been, well, sorted out. They – ' she paused as a thought struck her: 'Oh, goodness, it wasn't one of them, was it, who rang to tell you where I was?'

'No, no,' Rachel said emphatically. 'I worked it out through Ted Heywood, OK? At least you kept in touch with him! Yesterday I searched around Barossa Square without any luck. Then my luck changed and I saw your advert in that mini-supermarket. Honestly, I could just've easily missed it. Oh Mum, I – '

'So where'd you stay last night?' Janet Blythe cut in anxiously. 'London prices are ruinous for just about everything, so . . .'

'Oh, I'll tell you all that later, it's not important now,' said Rachel, glancing thankfully towards the door after hearing footsteps on the stairs: Pam had a heavy tread. She knew Mum would be horrified if she heard about the episode with El; and, anyway, Rachel wanted time to think more about that and about El herself. For some reason she knew she could forgive her for stealing her money. Money, now, didn't matter at all.

It was because she'd looked towards the door and her thoughts kept changing that she now noticed the shopping bags her mother had been carrying as she came into the sitting-room. Janet had dropped them just inside the doorway and no one had moved them.

'Mum, what did Pam mean when she said you'd got your outfit? Outfit for what? Are you planning to *stay* down here?'

Janet sighed again and seemed to Rachel to be confused rather than embarrassed; and Rachel wanted to say 'Don't run out on me again!' but just managed to remain silent, awaiting an explanation.

'Well,' Janet said slowly, 'this, you see, is the real reason I came to London. Helen is getting married and, well, I want to be there, of course. It's the – the least I can do for her after all these years apart.'

Rachel swallowed her surprise. But, before she could respond, Helen, as if on cue, came in, smiling and holding a tray of drinks.

'I thought you two might need a bit of space but I was missing you already,' she said but it was Rachel she was looking at before she lowered the tray onto the oak and glass coffee table. 'Sorry, but I couldn't help hearing what you said, Janet. Rachel, I was going to tell you myself but there was so much else to catch up on first.'

'Oh, Helen, that doesn't matter,' Rachel told her. She got up and went across to hug and kiss her and felt the tears start up in her eyes again. 'Congratulations, many, many congratulations! But when is it – oh, and who is it you're marrying?'

'Well, a patient, of course, who else do nurses marry!' Helen laughed. 'Not a patient now, though. I met him a year ago. His name's Brad – but no, he's not an American. Everybody seems to think anyone called

Brad has to be from the States. Brad Hedley, so I'll be Helen Hedley. I like the sound of that. How about you?'

'Yes, I do,' agreed Rachel. 'Almost as good as Blythe. Sounds shorter, doesn't it, but it's got the same number of letters.'

Janet was looking bemused, shaking her head in disbelief at something. Rachel, catching sight of her, was alarmed. 'Mum, what is it? What's wrong?'

'Oh, don't get worried, it's nothing that's wrong!' Janet said hurriedly. 'Just the opposite. The way you're talking now, you two, so naturally. You sound like sisters who've always known each other. Uncanny, really uncanny.'

'That's nice,' said Rachel, exchanging a grin with Helen that was practically conspiratorial.

'I can hardly believe this is happening, that you're so at ease with one another,' Janet added. 'It's the sort of thing I dreamed about for years. Well, day-dreamed, I suppose. But never, in my heart, believed it would come true. All this time I've felt like two one-parent families in one, mostly because Roy wasn't interested enough in you or me, Ray. But I needn't have been, I could have combined my families years ago. Instead, I've wasted years and years of my life.'

For the moment, no one could make any response. It was, Rachel knew, just what she herself had been thinking; but she couldn't say so because that would only have added to her mother's dejection.

'But it's going to work out now, Janet, you must know that,' said Helen, moving to sit beside her and take her hand. 'The future is what really matters, isn't it? You can just see that's going to be fine.'

'Exactly!' enthused Pam, coming in to seize a cup of tea and a couple of chocolate biscuits from the plate everyone else had ignored. 'Janet, my dear, I told you there was nothing to worry about, that it would all work out once the girls'd got together. Go on, tell me if I've got it wrong? Have I?'

Janet gently shook her head. 'Oh no. As usual, you've got it right, Pam. You've got most things right over the years, haven't you? "Keep in touch," you said, "but don't push it, don't push anything. Let it happen naturally." Always you've said that, and that's just how it's been.'

Listening to that exchange made Rachel realize how much contact there must have been over the years between her mother and Pam; and yet not a hint of it had ever seeped out at home. Even the prying, persistent Mrs Aries had known nothing of what Janet Blythe was up to or had been up to; and, from what Janet herself had disclosed, Rachel's father hadn't been aware of the truth, either. There was going to be a lot to talk about when they returned to Rocksea.

' – the wedding, too.' That was Pam speaking but because her mind had been elsewhere Rachel hadn't heard the rest.

'Oh, the wedding, that's what I really want to know about!' she exclaimed. 'You haven't told me yet when it is. Come on, I'm dying to know.'

'A fortnight on Saturday,' Helen replied. 'At a register office, not a church – neither of us wants that. And I want you to be my bridesmaid, Rachel. So will you? Please say yes.'

'Yes.'

She replied instinctively and so quickly that everyone laughed, some in relief, some in surprise.

'Wonderful!' Helen exclaimed. 'I was afraid it might be too soon to ask you. But there's so much I want to share with you, Rachel, and everything's happening so fast. I can hardly keep up with it myself. So it must be bewildering for you.'

Rachel nodded. 'I suppose it is. But I think I'm learning to cope with anything these days. I mean, I have to!'

Helen's expression was changing again after she'd glanced at Janet and Pam and seen their reactions. 'There is something else, Rachel, that you might as well hear now as later. I don't want any more secrets, I want us to share everything that can be shared.'

She paused, the serious expression still on her face.

'Something else?' Rachel asked, thoroughly bemused now. 'There can't be!'

'There is,' said Helen, sitting beside Rachel and putting her arm round her shoulders. 'I'm having a baby. Not for six months yet but, well, it's on its way.'

Rachel cried. She couldn't stop herself. She was crying with relief and amazement and sheer pleasure. In a moment or two she managed to say: 'So I have a sister – and I'm going to be a bridesmaid – and now I'm an aunt as well!'

'An aunt-to-be, to be accurate,' Helen observed cautiously. 'If all goes well . . . She, or he, will be born in Nottinghamshire because that's where Brad and I are going to live. That's where his new job is and we'll be moving next month. So – '

'Oh, that'll be much nearer us in Rocksea,' remarked Rachel, recovering quickly again. 'That's nice because we'll be able to see you more often.'

'I'm so glad you said that,' said Helen, hugging her. 'I think there's so much for us to look forward to, all of us.'

'I second that,' Rachel grinned through her tears. 'Lots and lots to look forward to.'

Faber Teenage Fiction
Other titles by Michael Hardcastle

Kickback

When the highly-strung race-horse Mantola disappears from Tildown House, only Ros seems determined to find him at any cost . . . 'The gripping tale of Mantola's rescue and Michael Hardcastle's realistic account of the horse-racing world make this a compelling read for horse and adventure lovers alike.' Madeleine Cassell, aged 14

Quake

Voted one of the best children's books of the year when it first appeared in 1988, Quake is an alarmingly vivid and convincing impression of what an earthquake could mean for an ordinary Midlands town. 'The reader is inextricably drawn into the panic and chaos.' *Times Educational Supplement*